PRIMARY WISDOM

THOMAS KOLP

outskirts press

Primary Wisdom

v2.0

This is a work of fiction. Names, characters, businesses, places, events, locales, and incidents are either the products of the author's imagination or used in a fictitious manner. Any resemblance to actual persons, living or dead, or actual events is purely coincidental.

Outskirts Press, Inc.
http://www.outskirtspress.com

ISBN: 978-1-9772-4802-2

Library of Congress Control Number: 2021922115

PRINTED IN THE UNITED STATES OF AMERICA

TABLE OF CONTENTS

PROLOGUE

I write this book in honor of the field general and the army nurse, the senator and the town priest, and for all of the teachers, coaches, and volunteers who possess the courage and resolve to selflessly serve others for at least one day.

"The end is the beginning; the beginning the end, and neither is either."

—Robert Ruhl

MILITARY OFFICER DESIGNATIONS

Pay Grade	U.S. Navy	U.S. Marine Corps
O-1	Ensign, ENS	Second Lieutenant, 2ndLT
O-2	Lieutenant Junior Grade, LTJG	First Lieutenant, 1stLT
O-3	Lieutenant, LT	Captain, CPT
O-4	Lieutenant Commander, LCDR	Major, MAJ
O-5	Commander, CDR	Lieutenant Colonel, LTCOL
O-6	Captain, CPT	Colonel, COL
O-7	Rear Admiral, RADM 1 Star	Brigadier General, BGEN
O-8	RADM Upper Half, RADM 2 Stars	Major General, MAJGEN
O-9	Vice Admiral, VADM 3 Stars	Lieutenant General, LTGEN
O-10	Admiral, ADM 4 Stars	General, GEN

CHAPTER 1

COMPLETION

"Wake up, Ruddster, it's graduation day," Marwinn barked as he rocked my bed with his knee.

I managed to open my eyes to a full-blown squint.

"No thanks, last duty, last night, and last call at Trader Jon's" was my groggy response.

"Yeah, I know, like I didn't hear you bumble in and bounce off a few walls last night at about 2 a.m."

"Pound sand, Marwinn, I'm not getting up. Let me know, though, if there are any babes on base. Have fun at work… " I think I managed to croak.

"Okay, numb nuts, suit yourself."

Mark Marwinn was my best friend and complete confidant. We were now roommates in a two-bedroom apartment near Pensacola Beach. We went to and through the University of Colorado together via Navy ROTC. We studied, cheated, and completely trusted each other as only brotherly criminals could. There still exists a very real bond and honor amongst us today, some twenty years later. No request by either of us would go unconsidered. I am lucky and grateful for his unwavering friendship and understanding.

I think I heard Marwinn say, "All right, this is your last chance, Rudd. I'm leaving in fifteen minutes to go to the selection brief. Would you like to come or should I just cover for you, AGAIN?"

The SELECTION brief? What the fah? Still foggy. The list doesn't come out until 1500, and the brief was just before that. Brain confusion, head pain.

I uttered, "The list?"

Mark continued to harass me. "Yeah, the new skipper changed the brief to 0800, not that you have ever noticed or cared enough to give one and a half shits about anything, much less your career," replied Marwinn as he sarcastically chomped on toast or more likely an English muffin.

New COs, short for Commanding Officers, the bane of my existence. They will always change things just for the sake of change. As if to ensure you know, "There's a new sheriff in town, and I think it's best you boys and girls play by my new sheriff rules"...motherfucking, fuck-faced dickheads, I solemnly thought to myself.

I was still fuzzy, but the list and the selection brief were big deals. The list was what we most cared about. It determined one's fate after completion of the U.S. Navy's Primary Flight Training. First and foremost, your name on the list meant you passed and graduated the second phase of Navy Flight School. It took all of my being to set aside my immaturity and propensity to drink too much beer to focus enough to pass. I spent many restless nights studying and working up the courage to succeed and present myself with the intelligence, organization, and confidence necessary to complete the syllabus. I was humbled.

Furthermore, the list indicates your path after Primary Flight Training. Simply, based on one's grades in "Primary" and the "Needs of the Navy and Marine Corps" (all Marine Corps pilots are required to earn Navy Wings), one would be selected to continue flight training for jets, E-2/C-2s, props, or helicopters. Coast Guard pilots also earn their wings via the Navy.

Jets: Obvious. F-14s, F-18s, S-3s, A-6s...missile-, bomb-, bullet-, and torpedo-laden aircraft carrier-based bad asses.

Props: Relatively uncool land-based P3s and C130s... surveillance and cargo machines. Per-diem extra cash collectors for their pilots though.

Helos: The much feared, truly needed, and wrongfully maligned helicopters of the U.S. Navy, Marine Corps, and Coast Guard.

E-2/C-2s get an honorable hooray as other. E-2 *Hawkeye* guys kick ass. They take tons of guff for the airplane they fly; that is an ugly twin engine turbo-prop with a large AWACS type radar dome on top of the airplane. They then adeptly slam this miserably yawing, huge twin propeller-driven machine onto the deck of a pitching ship with alacrity. Kick unrecognized ass! The C-2 guys do the same, except they don't stay on the aircraft carrier for six months (more like a day or two at the most) and they don't have that annoying reconnaissance radome on top of their aircraft. We navy folks call this mail, parts, and cargo delivery aircraft the "Cod."

Somehow, the words *selection* and *graduation* forced me out of bed. I saw my alarm clock, 0716, crap. I moved to the bathroom in a fog. I peed. I then moved to the sink and looked at myself in the mirror with disdain, true self-hate. I had been here before after too many beers. I noticed my headache. I then goofed with my way-too-short sandy brown hair as if it mattered. I of course checked the two scars on my face, and disgustedly noticed my red, white, and blue patriotic eyes. I squeezed some paste onto my toothbrush and hit the vacant spot where there used to be a tooth. Ooh, tender.

I recalled the day I lost that tooth. It was a Friday and a graduation day.

CHAPTER 2

VIPER

We had just completed Aviation Indoctrination. Say, that rhymes. Here, I met my peers. After many graduations and commissioning ceremonies, the Navy, Marine Corps, and Coast Guard assembles its officers selected to operate its aircraft and their associated systems. Some of us would become pilots and some naval flight officers or NFOs. NFOs are bombardiers, navigators, and mission specialists who deliver the goods and operate integral aircraft functions and systems. We came from all avenues. Some had the luxury of a degree from the vaunted United States Naval Academy. Some of us came from ROTC, some from AOCS, and a few had been prior-enlisted and then managed to complete college and become an officer. Then, through various programs, these chosen sweeties got a chance to fly for the Navy or Marine Corps. We all held the dreams and promise of Navy Wings. Take a guess as to which officers I admire most.

Back then, I assumed that the "Best of the Best" came from the academy. They generally were great high school students, community volunteers, and athletes, and they proudly and properly earned their appointments to the USNA. I say appointments because you literally have to be recommended and then appointed through a competitive process to a US Service Academy by a United States congressman, senator, vice president, or the president himself. These specially chosen underclassmen then go on to earn an Ivy League-worthy education. I was in ROTC in college, a Reserve Officer Training Corps type. Just the name with Reserve in it makes you feel like a second-rate turd. But, nonetheless, the program provides scholarships for students and officers to the military through a litany of U.S. universities. The Aviation Officer Candidate School (AOCS) also sent officers to the flight program. These idiots paid for their own college degree and then joined the Navy or USMC afterward. They then endured several months of hell just to try to become an officer and hopefully a pilot. These were the Richard Gere types as in *An Officer and a Gentleman*. I just called them Dicks as this is short for Richards. Finally, the Missies (short for miscellaneous officers) rounded out the group. These were the officers who were prior-enlisted personnel, former ship drivers, admirals' assistants, and, in general, all-around pains in all asses with too long and exhausting stories to hear or tell.

As for the guess...back then I was too arrogant to truly care, but as I said earlier, I gave the edge to the Naval Academy pukes. Today, I equally respect all of the men and women who have the gumption, strength, and selfless ignorance to attempt any military program. So getting back to it, the Navy initially sent all of these candidates to AI, that is Aviation Indoctrination.

As I write, I continuously think of how to address the United States Marine Corps, the USMC. Please just know that although I was a Navy screw, I still respect the uglies of the world...the God-blessed Marines. Talk about some guys who just don't care about anyone or anything outside of their immediate realm, except for probably the Constitution of the United States, and, possibly, their immediate families. I understand their militant outlook and their blasé thoughts of the Navy. I love their staunch demeanor and unstoppable ooh-rah enthusiasm. They have hideous uniforms, full of symbolism, that they so proudly don.

Sorry for the digression.

Anyway, we the student naval aviators (SNAs), the pilot wannabe portion of the AI students, were all assembled in an auditorium at Naval Air Station Pensacola, Florida. Admiral Watson himself would brief us after we completed phase one of Navy Flight School—Aviation Indoctrination.

AI was a hoot.

AI was a six-week-long welcome-to-naval aviation program that was kind of like summer camp. The best parts were after work hours. The P-Cola golf course and Officers Club were unmatched. Chicks, booze, and unfounded arrogance abounded. The real tragedy here was that my peers and I were mere ensigns and flight students and too starry-eyed on thoughts of flying airplanes to notice our most fortune circumstances. So we engaged in physical training continuously, golfed once, and knocked back a few at the O club, but never really took advantage of these sweet facilities. We were too cool and too stupid. We did, however, menace Pensacola at large and hit the bars on weekends. We frequented Trader Jon's, The Flora-Bama, The Sand Shaker, McGuire's, Wrong-Way Finnegan's, et cetera. More on these later.

So, getting back on track, Aviation Indoctrination consisted of a ton of physical activity, some classroom work, and operational weirdness. As for the physical activity, we had to swim what seemed like every day, practice on the obstacle course a la the *Officer and a Gentleman* movie, stretch, run, do calisthenics, and box. Yes, box like Rocky Balboa.

The classwork was surprisingly enjoyable. It was the part of the day where we got to stop sweating, literally. We listened to lectures, studied, and were tested on salient versions of meteorology, aeronautics, and navigation, and we relished lunch breaks between classes. We got up early for a mandatory run, workout, or swim. We actually looked forward to a shower and then putting on the khaki uniform in which to continue sweating. We were brainwashed, super-motivated dorks.

I was academically average. I was an idiot. I knew nothing of the Commodore's List nor the Admiral's List, which indicated graduating with honors. I truly and intentionally selected some wrong answers because I had "the gouge" and I didn't want to make it too obvious. The "gouge" was and still is, simply, answers and, more importantly, the previously asked questions as recalled by students. Great students and friends shared the knowledge of their experience, and there was no guarantee that tests wouldn't be changed. One still needed to genuinely learn the information or just "die by the gouge." However, in my super-motivated stupidity, I chose to get less than 100 percent. I felt some kind of moral obligation to not cheat. I had a 98.6 percent average in academics. I remember because one, it is normal body temperature; two, it was the house average; and three, because it grinds at me to this very day that I could have done better.

So we went on.

I enjoyed this summer camp. I continued my friendships with Marwinn and Petey. I met Harry, Farts, and many others whom I would eventually regard as supportive friends and role models.

Petey, Greg Van Piederson, Mark Marwinn, and I were friends and students at the University of Colorado, Boulder. We were all in the Navy ROTC there. We played sports together and compared notes on all subjects, including women, classwork, ski areas, beer, et cetera, and we quickly became close friends.

Harry Babcock and Gary "Farts" McSorley were new buddies to us and lived across the hall from Marwinn and me in an apartment in Gulf Breeze, Florida. They were ROTC lads from USC, SoCal Trojans. We were living large in the minds of twenty-two-year-old morons. We were seated near each other when...

"Attention on deck!" the admiral's loop shouted. The loop was and always will be the admiral's primary assistant. The loop accompanies the admiral constantly and is so nicknamed for the decorative gilded loop of rope he wears upon his left shoulder. In this case the rope was draped over a black and gold, two-and-a-half-striped and starred navy lieutenant-commander shoulder board. This rope is called an aiguillette in military terms, and I think it is a decorative symbol of an admiral's or general's aide assisting with his gear, especially in battle. I wondered how this worked out for, say...General Custer's kiss-ass assistant.

Anyway, the attention call startles everyone and always effectively serves its purpose. That is to end the banter and silence the audience so the dignitary can have the floor. We all snapped to our feet, chests out, guts in, eyes to the horizon, arms to the side, thumbs to pant seams, slightly curled fingers, and most importantly, shut the hell up immediately. The admiral and his loop walked briskly down the aisle in reverent silence, and His Magnificence took the podium.

The admiral took his hat from beneath his folded arm and handed it to LCDR Loop.

"Good morning, ladies and gentlemen, my name is Charlie Watson, call sign Viper, and I am your chief of Naval Education and Training," the two-star admiral before us stated. "At ease, please."

We all sat down but continued to gaze upon him with awe.

He was a thin, sinewy, super-fit late forty-something

and previous two-time Blue Angel, his second tour as their CO. Even I knew of him. Everyone and anyone remotely involved with aviation in general knew of Viper Watson. He also was a Vietnam fighter pilot and ace. An ace has at least five confirmed enemy aerial kills. All of those dogfights, the G's, the sweat, and oh my, where does he hide his enormous testicles? I thought to myself. He and his loop were dressed in Tropical Whites, the short-sleeved, open-collared summer uniform. They wore bar ribbons and nameplates. The admiral had gorgeous, glimmering gold shoulder boards with two silver stars on each. True to his dignified and quiet, confident persona, he never made mention of his heroism and always played it down when harassed by the media. I remember him deflecting the credit by telling one such interviewer on TV that the real heroes were the ship and submarine drivers, the mechanics, grunts, and weapons loaders, and by God the entire U.S. Military that made his job so easy. Yeah, I don't think wartime F-4 Phantoms and the word "easy" are synonymous. Maybe some word that embodies courage, terror, confidence, and doubt simultaneously would be more appropriate?

Viper continued in his deep, throaty, and no-nonsense voice. "Congratulations on your completion of Aviation Indoctrination. I know it seems like a small step on your journey to Navy Wings, but you have already endured a myriad of physical and mental challenges. You have been turned upside down underwater while strapped into the helo and Dilbert dunkers in flight gear and boots. You escaped. You passed. You hit the obstacle course with rigor and vigor, learned several swim strokes, were picked up and dropped back into Pensacola Bay by a helicopter, completed survival training in the woods, became POWs, fought each other with boxing gloves, PT'd every day, and hit the books. Yes, men, congratulations are due; you have graduated phase one of Navy Flight School."

A marine student yelled, "Ooh-rah!" Viper smiled. Some of us cheered, some laughed.

The admiral paused and I reminisced.

The helo dunker simulated a helicopter crash into a deep, cold, and dark swimming pool. It slowly sank and turned upside down as it submerged. The Dilbert dunker was the fighter jet crash device that violently flipped upside down into the water, literally tail over nose. For both, we were strapped into the cockpit in full flight gear including a flight suit, survival vest, gloves, boots, and helmet. I got water in my ears and up my nose.

We called survival training "starvival" as there was very little to eat for our three days in the woods. Apparently one can make a tent and sleeping bag out of a parachute. Butt cold though. This phase ended with a day and a half of incarceration by a pseudo-Russian enemy, played well by U.S. Military men and women.

As for the boxing, some lanky prior Golden Gloves graduate hit me right through my protective, puffed vinyl face guard with a compact and powerful right uppercut that made it to my chin. I blacked out. The only reason I could still stand was that I grabbed the ropes as my knees went weak and my world went dark and dizzy. My jaw was sore for three weeks. I made it through a round and a half with that animal, and the instructor graciously passed me and ended the fight after my TKO. I felt true humiliation, but no hard feelings. He was just plain better than I was. Congratulations are due to Ensign Pete Marozic.

The books...yeah.

We quieted ourselves and the admiral continued

his speech. "Consider this, men." He looked to his loop, who provided him with a clipboard. He put on reading glasses, glanced up, and paused for effect. "Twenty-eight medical disqualifications of prospective student naval aviators (SNAs). Twenty-eight officers who will not go to pilot school. Your class had not even started AI, and you already lost twenty-eight good men and women. Six more were removed for cheating, failing the O course, and voluntary separation. Four academic failures and eight physical injuries are preventing your classmates from continuing in the program. They are being evaluated, and these twelve may or may not return to SNA status. How many do we have here today, Jimmy?"

"Eighty-six," Lieutenant Commander loop responded. "So, doing the math we have eighty-six still going out of one hundred and thirty-two."

"Thanks, Jimmy."

The numbers were sobering. Sure, we knew of one or two stories of somebody having academic trouble, and the medical standards are rigid, but we were all surprised to hear that over one-third were gone.

"The Navy and Marine Corps need pilots, and it is my

job to provide them." Viper's face was turning crimson. "I have to do better. You have to do better! For those of you who think that AI was some sort of Mickey Mouse kiddie camp, think again. We might get two-thirds of your class to your first training ride in an airplane. Not just any airplane either. You will be cutting your teeth on the T-34C *Turbo Mentor*, a complex small beast. It is fully aerobatic and a complicated radio and instrument, jet-powered machine. Oh yeah, we put a propeller on it, too, to make you guys and gals pay attention to the plane's rudder. Therefore, I need your help. I need your dedication. I need you to do your best and to encourage and help your classmates as well. I need leaders. I need complete, competent officers. Now!"

The auditorium was silent. Admiral Watson removed his glasses, cleaned them, and set them on the podium. His deliberate actions were calculated and mesmerizing. He had our full attention.

Calmly, and in a solemn tone, he said, "Most all of the forty-six individuals that we just talked about would gladly trade places with any one of you today. I sincerely hope to return some of them to your ranks, and I truly want every officer in front of me to earn his or her Navy Wings. Unfortunately, this most probably will not be the case. The statistics tell me otherwise. Please stand up and look at the Marine or Navy officer beside you.

"Get face-to-face with a shipmate, damn it. Do it! I mean it!"

We stood and turned to look at the person next to each of us. As we gazed at each other, I really didn't believe what Viper was orating. He said simply that one day a long time ago, he was one of us, an ensign, eager to perform, yet tentative and unknowingly ignorant. I was literally looking down at a short ensign, last name GARCIA as stated on the generic black nameplate on her khaki uniform. The admiral babbled something about many of us experiencing life-changing events like marriage and children. He said that many of us would serve admirably and move on to civilian jobs. He said that he was proud that many of our nation's finest presidents and businessmen were born of our military. Blah, blah, blah, blah, blah. He then went on to say that one or more of us would die in the execution of our chosen duties.

"Be seated, ladies and gentlemen." He continued. "I

hate stats. They always seem to be stacked against me and the United States. We always seem to be fighting an uphill battle. There is always another enemy. To which I simply say, bring it on. We conquer internal problems daily, as does any good business or organization.

"We also go to war and win!

"For these two reasons, I need all of you to watch out for each other. Our jobs are dangerous enough already, so I don't need any additional problems caused by poor decisions. Please behave yourselves at the O Club and in town. Please don't mix it up with the townies and be respectful of the police force. Also, be a good wingman and a team player. Do your best to remove a peer from questionable situation. Be a good officer and citizen of Pensacola at large and this will go a long way in ensuring the safety of yourselves and fellow classmates. The statistics tell me that one or more of you will die in the execution of your duties as an officer in our military. So far we have lost aviation comrades every year of my military career. I want to change this unsettling trend and I need your help. I hope to see all of you through to bright, shiny gold wings and more. Let's focus on our responsibilities, encourage and help each other, and minimize failures, accidents, and tragedies. Think about it. Do it!

"I don't mean to scare you," Admiral Watson said in a low tone. "I mean to grab you by the balls and twist and whatever gets a girl's attention too! Be a good shipmate! That will be all."

LCDR Jimmy yelled, "Attention on deck," then Viper Watson and his loop departed but left the admiral's aura behind.

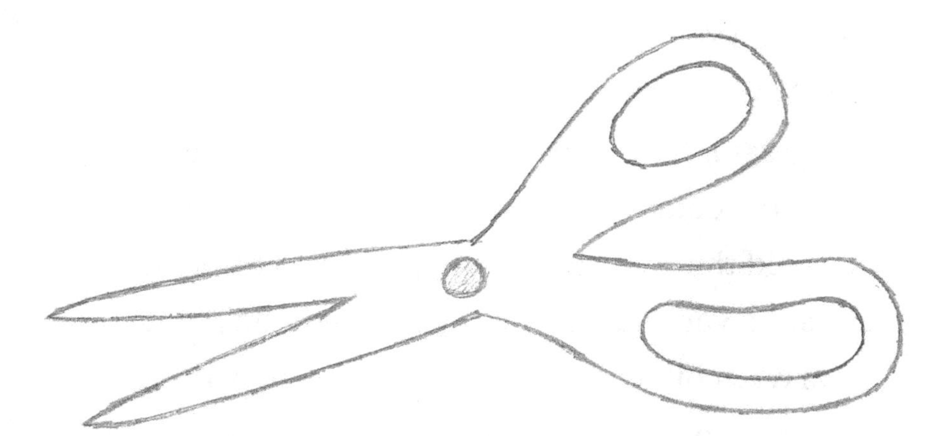

CHAPTER 3

TOMFOOLERY

We regrouped outside the auditorium across the street from Battalion 1, the AOCS outfit at Pensacola Naval Air Station, which is also called NAS P-cola and or just "main side" locally.

Petey left us to go take care of some administrative personal goods move hassle.

"Well, that was fun," I said to my buddies.

Marwinn chimed in, "Nothing like a good ass-chewing to start the day. Let's go to the Navy Exchange, our nifty on-base department and convenience store combined. Yay!"

Gary said, "Yeah, I need some stuff, so I'm down with that" in his California surfer dude kind of way.

I asked the two, "Have you guys been fitted for your flight suits yet?" just throwing a lure in the pond.

Marwinn bit as I knew he would as he was most aggressive when meeting deadlines and requirements. "What now..." he said with inquisitive innocence stamped on his face.

"Yeah, you have to get fitted for a general size before you can go to supply to get your flight gear. They told us on the last day of Aero class. You were probably taking a crap, and I'm sure Farts was sleeping," I replied.

"General size? Whoa, dude," from Gary, the thin, six-foot, four-inch, brown-haired young adult specimen.

"Yep, you just go to the uniform shop in the exchange, and they have several flight suits with the arms and legs cut off so you can easily slip them on and off to determine your size. I guess they're most concerned about stocking the supply shop properly and also making sure that your zoom bag doesn't go up your ass when you sit down."

"Oh yeah, I'm sure that's it, you dirt ball," Marwinn quipped with a smirk.

"I already did my measurement. I'm a forty-two regular. What about you, Harry?" I said to authenticate my nonsense.

"Forty long for me," Harry said on cue as he was wicked smart and caught on to my ruse quickly. Harry was six foot two, also had dark brown hair, and was of average proportion. His sharp, discerning brown eyes under his bushy eyebrows missed nothing.

"Just go on in and tell them you need fitted, and they'll take care of you. It's no big deal. It only takes a minute or two," I said with nonchalant encouragement.

"All right, we got it. See you dudes later at the O club for lunch?" asked Gary.

"Twelve hundred. We're down," Harry chided with goofy, waving arms.

"Right on, Hairball," Farts replied as he elbowed Marwinn. "Let's get on it, man."

With the trap set, Harry and I went off to hit some golf balls at the base driving range before lunch.

Marwinn and Farts met us for lunch at the O Club at 1200. Mark was oddly pleasant and even bought lunch for the four of us. We all ordered the fried oyster po'boys with french fries, which was the house special of the day at the Pensacola Officer's Club. Gary regaled us with the tale of the half-hour-long episode of trying to explain the necessity of getting fitted in flight suits with the arms and legs cut off to the Philippine employees of the uniform shop at the Navy Exchange. We all laughed heartily as we chomped down the hoagies soaked in tartar sauce. Marwinn kept laughing when he asked Harry and myself how well we liked the taste of his boogers. We still don't know whether or not he was joking, and he won't tell us to this day. I didn't vomit but my stomach still feels queasy when I recall this grotesque and most unfortunate turn of events. I realized that it is difficult to differentiate the taste between the two, and now I don't care for oysters.

"Nicely done," I conceded to Marwinn to try to maintain some semblance of dignity.

We departed company for a 1400 report time for check-in briefs to our respective primary flight training squadrons.

CHAPTER 4

VT-3

I flossed my teeth while remembering my first day as a Red Knight in Training Squadron Three.

We were seated like schoolchildren on one-piece, uncomfortable chair-o-desks in some impossibly bland and plain yellowish beige room called a space in the military.

In walked Captain Ronald Franklin, USMC, to deliver our check-in brief. He was shorter, about five foot, eight inches, and uncharacteristically pudgy for a Marine, red-faced and smelly. He was soaked wet with sweat shining through his flight suit on this miserably hot, humid Friday in June at North Whiting Field in Milton, Florida.

He began, "Shut the fuck up, sit the fuck down, and listen, you grabasstic, somewhat educated, collegiate morons!"

I thought "attention on deck" would have been more appropriate, but his method worked just as well and supported his nickname "Frankenstein" amongst the flight students.

He continued, "Good afternoon, ladies. On time and no excuses. That's what I, the squadron, and the skipper expect of you. I am Captain Franklin, the flight officer for this squadron, and as such my focus is churning out quality pilots, and not listening to whiny, sniveling SNAs telling me stories about how they have to go home to tend to Grandma's crotch fungus. You are here for one reason, and that is to get X's. An X is a completed event, and we have here at Primary Flight Training Squadron Three what is known as the completion curve."

I made the mistake of making a joke in the middle of his speech. I simply whispered to Marwinn in my cartoon character Beavis voice, "Uh, an X means I scored."

"Who the fuck are you and what the fuck are you whispering to your boyfriend, you little faggot maggot, nerd turd, and berserk jerk? Stand up, son, now!" hollered Frankenstein.

I hopped up and at attention said, "Sir, Ensign Rudd, and I only said that an X has more than one meaning. Sir."

There was some rustling and a subdued chuckle or two, but I unwittingly gave Frankenstein what he wanted. I would be his example, prop and bitch.

He walked over to me and examined my big black name tag. He then told me and the class in a surprisingly calm voice, "Rudd, I own your ass. I don't care that you think an X is planting your dick in Suzy Rottencrotch or your boyfriend here. An X to me, here at VT-3, only means one thing, and that is a completed event. You will be reporting to me as long as you are below the line I was just talking about. You see, we have this completion curve which translates out about eight months, and as long as you are on or above the curve, you are on or ahead of schedule, and you are a relatively happy SNA. That is, you are completing your events on time and therefore the squadron is completing the required pilot training rate known as PTR. You know who cares about PTR? That would be the skipper, Lieutenant Colonel Snake Collens, USMC. Every fucking week the skipper puts his head all the way up my ass and whispers in my ear, why are these SNAs below the line? Then I have to say that one guy has a broken ankle, and another got arrested in town, and this moron Rudd makes jokes while I'm trying to pass on pertinent information. Et cetera, et cetera. Now you will stand at attention for the remainder of this brief, Rudd, and you will not be reporting for duties as an SNA but as the assistant schedule duty officer, working for me, and helping me schedule X's for your buddies here for one week. That will put you nicely below the line, and you will be seeing me weekly for progress counseling until you get yourself on or above the line. We expect y'all to study, show up fifteen minutes early for every function, and have good flights and get solid X's. That will keep you away from me and the aforementioned progress counseling. Y'all know that makes me happy because I have one less problem to deal with, and as you can see,

I already have my hands full with Rudd here."

I must say his southern drawl was entertaining. He kept our attention and we listened to his instructions. We were all to go to supply immediately after his brief and get flight gear issued. We would each get two flight suits, a helmet with a microphone, built-in earphones and day and night visors, an SV-2 (a big, bulky survival vest with a life preserver built in and a bunch of other cumbersome survival items, just in case we had to camp in a farmer's field or on Pensacola Beach until we were rescued), green Nomex flight gloves, heavy black leather un-cushioned boots, a shitty brown leather jacket that we thought was the coolest thing ever invented, an ugly pair of outdated sunglasses that were literally in the movie *The Right Stuff*, a knee board with a Velcro strap and a clip and light at the top of it, a flip book to hold flight and aircraft information, and an aviator's oxygen mask. They then gave each of us a nylon olive drab two-handled helmet bag that we crammed full of these items. They also handed us a set of dog tags complete with neck and toe chains.

We were to check the next day's flight schedule every day to see if we were to fly an event, attend class, or serve as a duty officer for the next day. For training flights we were to show up at the Field Operations Office at least fifteen minutes prior to brief time with all of the required flight gear.

"Now then, let's see what y'all are doing on Monday as I am kind enough not to schedule newbie nuggets for duty on their first weekend here," Frankenstein said while thumbing through the schedule.

"Most of you will be attending the Fam Indoc brief at 0800 until 1100 and the preflight/egress brief in the afternoon from 1230 to 1600. Some of you will then fly Fam 1 on Tuesday. The rest of you can count on Fam 1 on Wednesday or as soon as your on-wing instructor is available. Always be sure to find your name on the schedule on a daily basis. Check for flights, briefs, events, meetings, schoolhouse sessions, and duties. If you are not scheduled, you will be listed at the end, right chere, under the additional SNA list. Your name should always be on this schedule, and it is your duty to find it, every...fucking...day," he said slowly for dramatic effect.

He added, "You may also call the SDO, that is the squadron duty officer, and she can check the sked for you, but it is not her fault if you miss something; that would be on you. I want y'all to take a look as you leave to familiarize yourself with the document you will live by for the next six months or so. Also pick up one stack of books from the table over there on your way out and study the Familiarization Flight stage for Monday.

"That will be all, ladies, dismissed."

I still stood at attention, not sure if his "dismissed" applied to me or not. Captain Franklin noticed and told me, "Yeah, Rudd you too, getcha's on outta here. You can ignore the flight schedule for now as you will not be going with your buddies here next week. You will report to me in the squadron operations office as assistant skeds O at 0700 Monday morning."

I sheepishly looked over the schedule, took a stack of books, and left. I was embarrassed, angry, and bent.

Marwinn met me at my car and knew better than to start in on me. He gave me some space to cool and simply said, "Well, since you're driving let's get over to supply and pick up your forty-two regular flight suits and the rest of our gear."

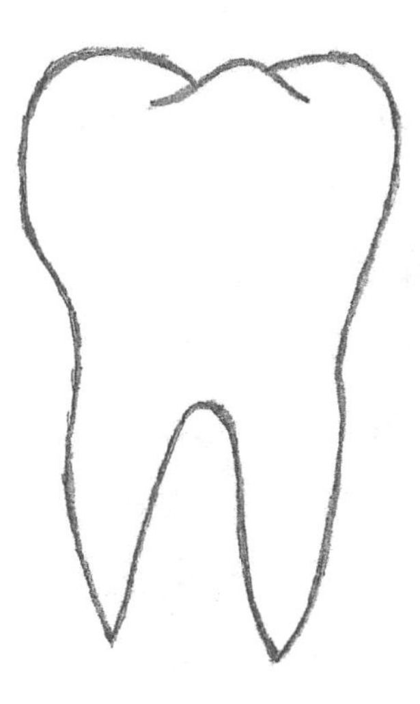

CHAPTER 5

NUMBER 19

My black Jeep Cherokee was packed with our flight gear and books. We were driving back to Pensacola from Milton in the early evening when we stopped for gas and beverages at the Tom Thumb convenience store. My nondescript car wasn't new but was well maintained and shiny and perhaps appeared upscale for the surroundings. I guess the same could be said for our rather plain beige khaki uniforms. I gave Marwinn a twenty-dollar bill and asked him to get us a six-pack of Bud Light for later and a couple of cold waters for the drive, and to get the rest in gas. We were parched.

I opened the fuel door on the rear left side of my jeep and noticed the depressed surroundings of Milton, Florida. The still air smelled moldy and the endless, scraggly pine and live oak trees were overgrown by moss. Most of the unpaved ground was a combination sand and clay with spotty patches of Bermuda and St. Augustine grass. I thought it weird that the ground could be so dry and the air so wet. The gas station and convenience store were dingy and tired. There was an old light blue, filthy Chevy Chevette next to me with a woman in flip-flops and cutoff blue jean shorts pumping fuel into it. She appeared young and pretty but unkempt and without the means to doll herself up. An old, noisy, used-to-be-white Ford pickup with two guys in it rumbled to the pump behind the Chevette and directly across from me. It caught my attention but not much of it.

A lanky southern young man in dirty jeans, a sleeveless undershirt, a John Deere ball cap, and cowboy boots got out of the driver's side of the truck and said, "Hey, Jolene, you're lookin' good. How 'bout we go out and shoot some pool tonight?"

“No way, Billy Ray. How about a nice dinner or fish fry or somethin’ and maybe some dancin’,” she said as she pushed her dark hair to the side of her stunningly beautiful pale face.

His enormous 280-pound buddy got out of the passenger side of the truck, slammed the door, resulting in a dusty rust cloud, and walked toward the small store.

Billy Ray shouted, “Hey, Ed Earl, get me some Skoal too.”

Ed Earl waved acknowledgment with his flabby right arm but never looked back.

Billy Ray went on. “Aw, come on now, I’m not made of money.”

Jolene retorted, “Well, then maybe you should get a real job instead of cuttin’ grass or workin’ on trucks and stuff. Maybe you could do somethin’ like that guy and do somethin’ respectable.”

I looked up and yep she was pointing to me and I thought, *Uh oh.*

Billy Ray caught me smiling at the attractive girl with awesome big blue eyes, firm breasts, and thin thighs and of course said, “Hey, what’re you looking at, peckerhead?”

I couldn't let it go. Dear God I wished I could have, but I had to say, "Dinner and dancing sounds pretty good to me, especially with someone as lovely as this young woman."

"You tryin' to hit on my girlfriend right here in front of me," asked Billy Ray.

I responded, "No, not at all. I was merely stating that I liked her suggestion, and perhaps you should honor her idea."

The tall, scrawny hick with long, greasy, light brown hair said, "Honor her idea?"

He was clearly angry and went off.

"You college boys roll into town and fly planes and stuff. Then y'all strut around in your pretty uniforms. Then you talk nice and fancy and steal our girls. Pisses me off. What do ya think about that, Mr. Respectable? Huh, ya faggot fuck?"

I responded, "Why don't you just relax, go home, bathe, comb your hair, trim your facial pubes, and brush your tooth. You then will be even more appealing, and the girls will like you too."

I had inserted the fuel nozzle into my car and was just turning to face him when I peripherally saw a silver flash. I heard a girl scream, "No!" I briefly saw Billy's angry grimace as the shining metal toe of his boot bit into the side of my already sore jaw. The tip of his shit-kicker sliced through my left cheek and crushed my lower middle molar. I felt extreme face and jaw pain and the wet heat of my gushing blood as my world was again going dark and dizzy. I dropped to my knees with my useless arms collapsing underneath my chest as I fell forward, rapping my forehead on the concrete curb of the gasoline island. I fantasized about dowsing Billy Ray in gas and lighting him on fire as I blacked out.

Apparently, Marwinn saw the event and took care of Billy Ray. Mark was a muscular six-foot, one-inch, 205-pound gym fanatic who liked to box. He grabbed Billy by the collar and rammed his back through the dirty glass of the old-fashioned gas pump. He then pulled him out and up on his dazed feet. Two quick left jabs and a right cross to his face later and Billy Ray was a bloody, confused mess. Billy was barely standing and wobbling when big fat Ed Earl dropped his bag of Mountain Dew and Skoal and threw a clumsy right at Marwinn. Mark easily saw it coming, ducked and buried his right knee into Ed's soft belly as he stumbled by.

The knee collapsed Ed Earl's abdomen, forced the air from his lungs, and made him throw up.

I'm told that in this mess of puke and blood, Jolene was the voice of reason. She screamed, "Y'all need to stop and somebody call an ambulance!"

The shop clerk came outside and shouted, "Everybody stop and simmer down. The cops are a comin'!"

The word "cops" made Billy Ray stumble to his truck. Ed Earl got off of all fours, left his pile of used corndogs, and while gasping for air through his drooling, portly, puke-ridden, bearded face, made his way to the passenger's seat.

The rusty, used-to-be-white, noisy truck sped off.

Jolene, Mark, and the store clerk told Deputy Sheriff Walsh their perceptions and fairly accurate versions of the whole fracas.

I woke up in an ambulance with another excruciatingly sore jaw.

And that was the graduation day on which I lost that tooth, I thought to myself as I avoided the gum hole and finished brushing my remaining teeth.

CHAPTER 6

ASDO

I walked into the squadron schedules office at 0645 on Monday morning. I sat in an inconspicuous chair near a corner of the plain, utilitarian room. There was a chalkboard and some sort of slot board on the big wall. There was a huge aviation type map of the US on the wall with the door. A wall of windows guaranteed heat on this already sultry June day. The back wall of the room had an old but operational two-foot, circular, three-handed clock, which noisily ticked off the seconds, adding to my anxiety. It seemed that each tick coincided with the throbbing pain on the left side of my face.

I looked up and I got him. He momentarily dropped his jaw, lost his military bearing, and had a genuine look of empathy when he first caught sight of me.

"Boy, what in *the* hell happened to you and why aren't you at sick bay right now?" asked a surprised and maybe even concerned Captain Franklin.

I popped up to attention and strained to say, "Sthir, Ensthign Rudd reporting ath ordered...sthir."

He walked over and closed the door. "At ease, Rudd, and start talking...slowly."

He set his mug of coffee on the large metal desk, walked to a far corner of the room so as to guarantee privacy, and motioned me to follow.

I explained the gas station incident and that I spent Friday night and some of Saturday in the Santa Rosa County emergency clinic. I told him about the stitches on the outside and inside of my cheek and how I got the massive, horizontal lump and another set of eight stitches on my forehead. I told him about my crushed left molar and that they did what they could at the clinic, but that it would need further evaluation from a dentist and maybe an oral surgeon. I told him that I was released early Saturday morning without signs of a concussion and that I was on a Tylenol and Motrin regimen to reduce swelling and relieve pain, but no prescription drugs. I told him that I figured I was in enough trouble already and that I did not want to fall further below the curve, and that I would most like to get on with my immediate mission of Primary Flight Training. He examined the purple, blue, black, and greenish yellow, swollen, and hot left side of my face. He squinted and winced at the ugly, stitched, large horizontal lump on my Cro-Magnon-looking forehead.

He was looking down and shaking his head and said, "Well, if this just don't beat all. Here it is Monday morning and I'm met by someone who looks more like Frankenstein than I ever have," indirectly acknowledging his nickname. "I'm supposed to have an able, clear-minded assistant, not a beat-to-shit moron. Damn it, boy, I just don't know what to do here. To me, you look like trouble, and I should therefore advocate your removal from flight training and, hell, maybe even go after your girlfriend, Marwinn too. The Navy doesn't like bad PR and just might discharge you two idiots."

"Goddamn it, don't do that, sthir," I begged in a low tone with a tear welling in my left eye.

He heard me and continued, reasoning and thinking it out as he spoke.

"Anyone else know about this yet, especially like admirals or the media?" he asked.

"No, sthir, not to my knowledge."

"And this is the first notification of the squadron?"

"Yes, sthir."

He mumbled, "Well, that's at least good."

I felt hope and a touch of relief. My second positive impression of Capt. Franklin of the morning, wow. Did I like this guy? Was he earning my admiration?

"Okay, Rudd, I'm going to give you a shot. If the sheriff's report plays out like you said, maybe this wasn't all your fault. You'll probably get a court date and we'll see how that all works out. In the meanwhile, this is how we're gonna play it. I'll go to the skipper and try to smooth things out a bit before you and your girlfriend Marwinn go to see him. If he doesn't call you into his office ASAFP, make an appointment with his secretary to see him, and explain what happened and, more importantly, tell him that you want to be here and do a good job. I respect that you came here, despite your injuries and overall stupidity, and I will allow you to serve your week of scheduling. Just try not to ooze or bleed on anything. You'll have to see our flight surgeon this week also, and get cleared to return to normal duty if the skipper allows it. You can do that toward the end of the week after you heal up a bit."

"Thank you, sthir, you're a quality human," I said in a quiet, sincere, and thankful tone.

"Yeah, well, don't tell anybody, because I prefer to be detached, misunderstood, and feared, like Mary Shelley's Frankenstein."

CHAPTER 7

LUCKY ME

0900 that same Monday morning.

"Lucky you," said Capt. Franklin as I was struggling to comply with the actual scheduling officer's directions. I was the assistant scheduling duty officer, not the actual scheduler, so my job was to assist in any and all ways and try to keep up with the frantic pace of the job at hand. That job was and probably still is to schedule X's.

"The skipper will see you now." Captain Franklin

showed me the way to Lieutenant Colonel Collens' office, and he joined me at attention in reporting as ordered.

The skipper's office was nice. It was spacious, cool, and comfortable. He had a large mahogany desk with a small US flag and his super cool nameplate, stating LTCOL Harold T. Collens with the Marine Corps eagle, globe, and anchor symbol on it. There were pictures on the walls of jets, helicopters, and even a navy ship. He had the US flag with the snake on it that said "Don't Tread on Me," hanging on the wall behind his desk. He also had a red leather swivel chair for himself and a brown leather couch and two simple brown wooden chairs across from his desk for visitors. The floor was hard, crappy, probably surplus tile, but the office was the best the squadron had and was formidably pleasant.

Frankenstein briefed me on the way over to talk minimally, answer questions, and not much else. I would gladly comply.

LTCOL Snake Collens started, "At ease and be seated." We sat in the two chairs slightly behind us. The skipper paced behind his desk with his hands folded under and his chin and his two index fingers pointing at his nose. He was a lean six-foot, two-inch tall, bald African American and he was ripped. He was an impressive physical specimen.

He began. "Captain Franklin has filled me in about your injuries and the *incident* that happened in town on your first day here. He told me that despite being banged up, you wish to proceed as a student naval aviator. I wanted to see for myself that you can function and that you do not need the kind of medical attention that would preclude you from duty. I understand that you cannot be qualified to fly at this moment, but that you can and want to stand office duty until you can. Is this correct, Ensign Rudd."

"Sir, yes, sir," I said slowly and carefully, striving for correct pronunciation.

He looked at me and assessed my broken face. He continued.

"I plan to talk to your compadre Ensign Marwinn and check with the Sheriff's Office myself to see what the ramifications of your *event* are. I expect you to comply with all legal requirements and to keep us apprised of your situation. I expect you to stay out of trouble. You are banned from the Tom Thumb store in question and for that matter all local business establishments in the Milton area. Take care of your personal needs and fuel up at main side or in Pensacola. Am I clear?"

"Yes, sir, crysthal." Oops, I thought to myself.

He raised an eyebrow and I could see that the skipper was operating with controlled anger. Was he mad at me or the townies? Probably both and the unpleasantries placed upon him to boot. He no doubt would talk to the sheriff and brief the admiral about me. Crap. He went on.

"I am putting my trust in Captain Franklin's recommendation and I will allow you to serve as he sees fit. You are on thin ice, Rudd, and you are on my personal list of probation. You've made my shit list, and that is not a good thing. The rut you are in is deep and lined with slime, making the climb out difficult and maybe impossible. Your job is to obey orders and keep your nose clean. I don't want any more negativity from you, and should I have occasion to see you again, Ensign Rudd, it better be to give you a medal! That is all, dismissed."

As we walked back to the scheduling office, I sheepishly asked if the skipper knew about my X comment last Friday. “No need, you’ve already one-upped yourself,” said Frankenstein. This guy was actually pretty cool. I began to respect him as somebody who truly leads by example, one of my very few personal tenets.

CHAPTER 8

A PHD

I worked hard and learned for my first two weeks at the squadron. I snagged grease pencils, erasers, lead pencils, pens, staples, hole punches, coffee, etc. I was the go-for, for whatever it was that the schedulers needed. I was lost and running every which way, like a lone rookie outfielder shagging batting practice balls on a minor league baseball team.

The scheduling crew was comprised of the scheduling officer, called "Skeds," and two enlisted Navy petty officers. Skeds was a Navy instructor pilot who was plenty angry and frustrated as he had three more months in this unenviable position due to his knee injury. He was rehabbing a torn right ACL he earned from pickup basketball. LT Gluck hobbled and grumbled around and was sufficient, I suppose. He continuously griped about the physical therapy that he endured every afternoon, Monday through Friday. He earned the call sign Lt. Grumpy or just Grumpy amongst the squadron.

Petty Officer First Class James "Buster" Winfield was the nuts, bolts, and brains of the operation. He was a super smart Navy yeoman. He was also pleasantly enjoying his shore duty and the warm Florida weather. I enjoyed his good humor, wit, and sarcasm. He mastered administrative duties, worked out every day, and would surely make chief petty officer early, his next anticipated rank.

Petty Officer Third Class Elizabeth Fox was just that. She was tall, thin, blonde, blue-eyed, and beautiful. We all noticed but were too intimidated by her looks to comment on them, and I certainly didn't want to risk any fraternization accusation. Hmph, another rhyme. She was twenty years old, bright, wore a smart uniform, and quizzed me about college application.

We all worked for Captain Franklin, the flight officer who in turn worked for the operations officer, who was the head of the Operations Department and was also known as the Operations Department head or the OPSO or just Ops. The other department heads were the safety, NATOPS, aircraft maintenance, administration officers and the first lieutenant, who was in charge of the buildings' and facilities' maintenance and the various squadron watches. The "First" had the most frustrating job and hence it went to some junior officer, usually whom the skipper didn't like. Most of these department heads were Navy lieutenant commanders or USMC majors and reported to the executive officer, or XO, who was Navy Commander Alex Smith, call sign Shooter, of course from the Smith and Wesson gun company, although I never confirmed any relation to either. The XO reported to the CO, who was Marine Lieutenant Colonel Collens.

I had the misfortune of being assigned to VT-3, which is the only squadron with Marine Corps and then Navy commanding officers flip-flopping every year, and accordingly the squadron was rife with hard-core Marine instructor pilots. Lucky me.

I found the whole structure confusing. We had to schedule the weekly department head meeting, and thus I was forced to learn the administration from bottom to top. All of these department heads had various junior officers beneath them. We also scheduled this whole gaggle for the weekly All Officers' Meeting, known as the AOM, an organizational foundation used throughout the Navy. This seemingly complicated but routine knowledge would prove helpful as my military career progressed.

I was busy. In addition to scheduling the meetings, watches, and aforementioned briefs and classes, we had to address the squadron's primary function, and that was to schedule and complete X's. While passing a class was technically an X in a box, an X was mostly considered a completed training flight of which there were about eighty-two sorties per day. These were comprised of both instructor and student training flights. The instructor flights were those for already-winged pilots who were being qualified to present the syllabus, and the student flights were for SNA instruction.

I was embroiled in my job and I was also scheduling

myself to see a doctor, dentist, and our flight surgeon. I had little time for chitchat and I was trying to hustle around and make up for my mistakes. I kept my mouth shut and ears open. I had just delivered two cups of coffee when Buster cornered me and said, "Smile a little, it's not so bad. I've been around the Navy a long time, and I've seen worse. These things pass. Think ahead a little, use your time here to your benefit. Find out what it is that these golden winged flyboys want you to know. You'll be fine."

I appreciated and took his advice. I learned to smile through the discomfort of the stitches. That damned number 19 tooth of the dental chart was another story. The dentist removed the stitches from my cheek and forehead too as a favor. He pulled what was left of the roots of number 19 and promised me another tooth in time. He was torn between trying a bridge or attaching a molar to some kind of screw or post. He said he would show my x-rays to some of his colleagues and come up with a treatment plan. LT Green was pleasant enough, but he did confide that he was fresh out of dental school, and he was excited that he would be a lieutenant commander in a week. He apparently had a lot on his plate too.

I watched as Grumpy and the petty officers developed the daily schedule. They first literally slotted all of the briefs and classes on the slot board for the day and week to come. They would then see which instructors and students were available to fly, and pair them for flights. The first launch was on the first fifteen-minute increment after sunrise and the last launch at 2045 local time. The squadron would get assigned two or three aircraft from the massive pool of T-34C Turbo-Mentor aircraft on every fifteen-minute increment between sunrise and 2045. This information came from the maintenance aircraft availability report, which I fetched first thing each morning.

Primary flight training was divided into stages. The familiarization stage was flown during daylight hours and was the student's initial introduction to basic flying. The precision aerobatic and formation stages were next, and also flown in daylight. Basic and radio instrument stages followed and could be flown day or night. Lastly the VFR night familiarization completed the aircraft training portions and would be flown after sunset. I was lost and intimidated.

I lunched outside in a picnic table area and watched as the multitude of T-34s taxied, took off, and recovered. I was told that the only airport busier than North Whiting Field in Milton, Florida, was O'Hare International in Chicago, fittingly named after Navy pilot and WWII hero Butch O'Hare. It seemed plausible. I learned the entry and exit points and taxi routes to and from the runways. I watched instructors teach and chastise. I eavesdropped on the briefing rooms and wrote down the questions and sometimes correct answers.

I became friendly with several instructors and I would try to get them slotted for the times and flights or "hops" they wanted. I studied and asked them questions about techniques and procedures.

I bought a cheap Mr. Coffee brewer from the exchange and donated it to the skeds office. I mostly did it for selfish reasons as I was tired of chasing back and forth to the wardroom for the gallons of coffee required to run the office. I bummed a small desk and set up cups, cream and sugar. I brought donuts on Mondays to ease the pain of the coming week.

The skeds crowd took to calling me Ensign College-boy as I helped them with their newfangled word processor, a rudimentary Apple computer. They were trying to transition from their tried-and-true grease and slot boards to a "computerized" schedule, but we really weren't close and we just used the Apple as a typewriter. I would take the typed schedule to the XO for approval every day and brief him on how many X's were scheduled and how many students would be completing training that week. Most importantly, I learned to brief him on his and the CO's events for the day and upcoming week. I sucked at all of this at first, but I learned quickly. The XO would confer with the skipper, revise once or twice, and then mercifully sign the document, completing my task and making it the official orders of the CO for the following day.

I managed to sneak off to the familiarization stage brief and completed the preflight qualification known as Fam Zero during my office stint.

I was just getting good at my administrative position when my office tenure abruptly ended. I was still missing a tooth, but medically cleared to fly. I served three weeks as the ASDO, and on Monday June 12, 1989, I was scheduled for Fam One with my on-wing instructor, Captain Ronald Franklin, USMC.

CHAPTER 9

KNOW IT ALL?

Familiarization flight zero is not a flight but a grip and grin. It is a meet your on-wing instructor session, a discussion of expectations, and you also accomplish a "preflight" together. Every pilot around the world preflights their aircraft before flying it. We check for damage, loose rivets, tire inflation, oxygen pressure, fuel and hydraulic leaks, oil and fuel quantity, battery connection, switch positions, etc. I had unknowingly accomplished the event and earned my first X about a week ago when Capt. Franklin wolfed down a sandwich and showed me around an airplane. We looked at the T-34C Turbo Mentor, and he pointed out most of the pertinent parts of the aircraft and its PT-6 small jet engine as well. The aircraft looked like a piston-driven propeller airplane but actually was powered by the PT-6 jet turbine engine via a complicated reduction gear box that winds up driving the propeller. My overall impression was that the plane was small with room for only two pilots who would sit in tandem. The plane was painted orange and white. I remember thinking but did not dare say, "Where's the yellow *Baby on Board* diamond sign?"

I didn't know it then, but Captain Franklin personally assigned students to their on-wing instructors. The on-wing phase was the first six flights in the airplane and thought of as absolutely critical. The SNA would receive consistent instruction from one person who would literally teach and mentor the student to perform in accordance with Naval Aviation. Most instructors would not qualify to be "on-wings" until about six months or so in the squadron. Some never make it. The relationship is borderline sacred, and the on-wing instructor is the SNA's counselor throughout primary flight training.

I was scheduled for Fam One, and we met at 0900 on Monday. I studied the books and memorized the procedures. Navy flying is procedural by nature and highly standardized. I learned in some class that this was a necessity and imperative for combat reliability. Every pilot should be procedurally identical so we can easily and interchangeably fly with each other.

I showed at 0845 with my gear and geared up to impress Capt. Franklin. I aced the brief. I knew the procedures for normal and emergency operations alike. I dashed off these checklists with impunity. I possessed the book knowledge of how to taxi, take off, climb, descend, speed change, and even some advanced emergency maneuvers like high and low altitude power losses, engine fire, chip light, and more! Boy, was I ready, until Frankenstein said, "Have you ever flown an airplane before?"

CHAPTER 10

UP, UP WE GO

I splashed water on my face in a desperate attempt to wake up and clear my head. I wiped it with the blue towel that was hanging on the short wall to the right of the sink. I thought about that first flight.

We left the briefing cubicle, exited our building, and walked over to the operational hangar known as the flight line. We hung our flight gear on some big hooks of a handmade piece-of-crap wooden rack. We went inside to a large office that smelled of grease and jet fuel.

Capt. Franklin gave the maintenance chief a stick of Beemans gum. The chief, standing behind a long counter, offered a friendly and perhaps knowing smile, took the gum, and handed Frankenstein a large three-ring binder, the maintenance log for our assigned aircraft.

The heavyset chief of maintenance said, “Fam One, huh?”

Franky replied, “Yeah, but don’t you worry now. I’ll be back in a coupla hours, and return your bird in good shape.”

Big “Bob,” according to his name patch, said, “Fair enough.”

We went to a twelve-foot-long, nipple-high, beat-up metal table against the wall across from the long counter, and Franky showed me stuff in the aircraft log book. I was already lost and overwhelmed by the noise and commotion that surrounded us like the twisted, tangled tent of a Boy Scout on his first try. He signed something. We left, gathered our flight gear, and started walking in the direction of Echo 514, our assigned T-34C for the flight, as indicated by yet another grease board diagram that hung prominently in the “office” we just departed.

My first ride in a Navy airplane! I was hoping for a shiny, new one, but it looked more like the grandmother of an old witch. E 514 was dirty, splotched, and appeared tired. Franky was yelling at me, but I couldn't hear a damn thing through my ear muffs and over the continuous roar of prop and jet noise from other airplanes taxiing about. I was standing in front of the prop and looking around not in a daze but in ignorance of what to do next. He caught my eye and waved me over to the left wing root. He put his gear down in the shade provided by the aircraft and I did the same. I followed and watched as we—but mostly he—conducted the exterior preflight. I did remember from our brief to stay tight to the airplane so as not to get run over by ground equipment or mutilated by a spinning propeller.

We fastened the last exterior compartment of our inspection and picked up our flight gear. We donned our survival vests, the SV-2s. We climbed up the port side and onto the black non-skid sandpapery walkway of the left wing which spanned from leading edge to the back of the wing along the canopy. Franky told me to never step on the pretty, painted part of the wing. He showed me how to attach and stow my oxygen mask and how to put my helmet on the rail of the canopy. We stowed checklists, my kneeboard, and my water bottle in a little niche between some radios on the right side of the cockpit. I climbed in and sat down in the front seat of the two-man tandem cockpit. Franky ensured that I attached the miserably uncomfortable parachute correctly, and that I fastened the five-point harness, told me to put on my helmet, said good luck, slapped my left shoulder twice, reached in, and flipped a switch up, then disappeared to the rear seat of the aircraft.

Here I was, wearing gloves, a full-length dark green Nomex flight suit, a cumbersome SV-2, dog tags, and combat boots. I was sweating bullets or maybe nuclear missiles on a humid 92 Fahrenheit degree day with the relentless sun pounding away at us. We were at least an hour into the hop and we essentially had done nothing yet. *Maybe this isn't for me; maybe I just can't do it. What the fuck am I doing here? Have I felt like this before? Maybe...*

"Check, check," I heard through the earphones of my helmet. I pressed the toggle on the power control lever down and replied, "Check?" in a squeaky, less than confident voice.

"Good, we're talking. That was the main battery that I switched on, which is a necessity for our inter phone communication. Most of you newbies forget or don't know to turn it on, so I gave you a little freebie to get us headed in the proper die-rection, as this is your first time flyin' and all."

His southern voice was now slow and soothing. I was grateful for it. At this point I would need all the help I could get.

He continued, "Now then, how about we start this thing up so ins we can turn on the air conditioner."

My voice unsteady, I managed to plod through the checklists and ready the airplane for start. I gave the fire guard, a Navy enlisted man posted in front of our plane with a tall red extinguisher on two wheels and a skid, a thumbs-up. The man wearing goggles and a helmet pointed at the nose of the airplane with his left hand and started making circles in the air with his right. I flipped the start switch up with my left hand and I heard some ticking, and the prop started to turn. I was supposed to check for 10 to 12 percent N2 on a gauge, but I was lost and forgot what to do next. Luckily, the fuel lever magically came out of its detent and the start continued. The motor sounded only like a dull hum. Next the condition lever again came full forward on its own, and I heard the "eeeeyow" sound of the propeller coming up to speed, and the engine stabilized at idle. I suddenly realized that Captain Franklin was moving the lever, that he had a full set of interconnected controls in the back seat, and I was grateful that he would use them to keep us safe.

"Hey, do you see that switch down between your legs that says Air Con?" asked the voice inside my helmet.

"Yee-eess, sir," I replied with my voice cracking like I was revisiting puberty.

Franky then said, "Go ahead and switch that on. Ahhh, that helps. Now then, I will be doing most of the flying today and demonstrating the operation and capabilities of this ol' bird. I suggest that first you take a drink of water, so as to keep your brain lubricated; then your job is to pay attention and learn to do what I am doin'."

He said, "I have the controls," and he proceeded to show me some of the finest flying I have ever had the privilege to experience. I know that I was new and starry-eyed, but even now after tens of thousands of hours of pilotage, I remember his effortless, quiet confidence and his ability to finesse that old nag into feats of beauty. I also remember incessant chatter on the radios and constant motion of vehicles and airplanes around us, especially on the ground. What a zoo.

Captain Franklin did not inundate me with procedures while in the cockpit. He was mostly quiet about the particulars of controlling the aircraft. He did stress his big three.

1. Aviate: Operate the "killing machine" safely at all times.
2. Navigate: Look outside a lot and know where you are going.
3. Communicate: Talk.

He told me that the big three must be done continuously and in order.

He demonstrated the basics of taxi, takeoff, climb, cruise, descent, and landing. He also showed me the cool stuff. He demoed a spin, ninety-degree angle of bank wingovers, a vertical loop, half and full Cuban Eights, an Immelmann, a split S, and aileron, and barrel rolls. He also showed me the effects of positive, negative, and zero gravitational forces. He pushed the airplane over into a parabolic arc and showed me my water bottle and flight manual as it floated around the cockpit as if we were in outer space. He stressed the importance of securing loose items. He told me to relax and enjoy the view and then pulled some sudden G's. I grayed out.

He orated only key points about each maneuver.

He also let me fly some, and to my surprise I could control the three-dimensional, wicked little beast a little.

We secured E 514 in the chocks, returned it to the now cheerful, rotund maintenance chief. We headed back to a cubicle in the Ops building now assigned to the Red Knights of Primary Training Squadron Three.

CHAPTER 11

DEBRIEF

"Now then, what did ya think?" asked my on-wing instructor.

"Well, sir, I felt as though I stayed in tune, flew okay, and learned quite a bit from one of the world's greatest military aviators."

Captain Franklin continued, "Did you know that I was an English major at my beloved Tulane University?"

"No, sir."

"Well, I was, and one of the things I learned there

was to recognize top-notch, first-class, grade-A, high-quality bullshit. Now why don't you set aside what you're trying to feed me and tell me how you really felt, and hell, maybe even how you are feelin' right the freak now."

I considered his request for a moment and silently decided, what the hell, go for broke, this may have been my first and last flight in a Navy plane. I spilled my guts.

"I was lost. I was overmatched. I was hot, literally. One time when you told me to relax, everything went into black and white with the black crowding in like a big circle from outside in. I didn't know what to say or do for most, heck, all of the flight. I was confused. As for now, I feel defeated. I don't know that I can safely perform as you did today, ever. I'm hot, physically and mentally exhausted, maybe a little embarrassed, and beaten."

"Now that's more like it," he said with renewed enthusiasm. "If this was easy, anyone could do it. I will teach you and you will learn. You will learn to compartmentalize your head wounds, the sweat in your eyes, and your personal issues. There ain't no cryin' in flyin'. You will learn to recognize but not be overcome by the noise and events around you. And, all the while, you will be operating the airplane in an adept and safe manner. You know all those procedures you so prettily spouted off before we went flying? You probably didn't think of them much while we were in the killing machine. Well, I was and I wasn't. They have become innate to my being while I act as the pilot in command. Heck, for a simple takeoff, I know that with clearance from the tower, you check the runway clear, turn the anti-collision strobes on, align the aircraft on centerline, hold brake pressure, advance the throttle to five hundred to five hundred and fifty foot-pounds of torque, check instruments, heels to the deck, advance the throttle takeoff power, hold centerline with primarily right rudder and forward stick pressure, but adjust as necessary with rudder and aileron for wind, rotate the airplane with light back stick at ninety knots, and let her fly off as you slowly rotate to the initial climb nose high altitude, and at four hundred feet turn to assign the heading. Then it's just gear up, flaps up, after takeoff checklist. The most important part of all of that, however, is that I'm simultaneously looking outside and making sure we're not going to hit anybody or anything. You got any questions?"

"Yes sir. 'Killing machine'? It seems a little scary and overly dramatic."

"Good, I'm glad it got your attention, because that's exactly what it is. Just like a car or motorcycle, these wonderful machines are convenient and fun when used properly, but when we get lazy or stupid, they kill us, literally. Never forget that they are cold, heartless chunks of metal worthy of our respect and diligence.

"Oh, and I set you up for that gray-out. Some of your compadres black out. I just wanted to show you the importance of utilizing your hook maneuver and the necessity to stay awake while flying. Also your bloodshot eyes will recover in a couple of days. They're just a result of the negative G's when all your blood rushes on up into your otherwise empty head."

The hook maneuver is bearing down and flexing the muscles in your legs and abdomen in order to force blood to the brain so as not to gray or black out. It is suggested to forcibly say "hook" as a technique for positive G survival.

Captain Franklin then talked about our next flight together, Fam-Two. He said it would be tomorrow or the next day and reminded me to check the sked daily. He gave me three assignments in addition to studying the operational items for Fam-Two. He told me about the "Immortality of Verse," that is in olden times folks like Socrates and Shakespeare would write things down so that their words would live on after they themselves suffered their physical deaths.

He quipped, "So write these down. It'll last longer, dummy."

I wrote:

1. Think about the big three, Aviate: Navigate, Communicate.
2. Practice in the preflight bird (an airplane made available to SNAs with the battery disconnected so we could practice throwing switches and moving the flight controls) so as to become a procedural pilot of action and not words.
3. Stay physically and mentally healthy. Exercise, eat right, forgive yourself for your egregious abominations committed today, and move on.

"One more thing there, Ruddster. Never ask about grades in the debrief. Most instructors will tell you how you did or fill out the form right in front of you. It is our job as instructors to evaluate and record your performance, and we will do just that after every flight. You can always look at your training jacket and see how you are doing. Eh, once every coupla weeks should do, mostly to make sure your records are up to date. As for today, two above hop. You were a clueless, complete primate from the flight line clear through to parking the bird, and that is house average for your first flight. You did have excellent book knowledge in the pre-brief, and that's an A for effort. Do you have any questions?"

I asked with a humble, puzzled expression, "Two above averages, sir?"

He said, "Now I just told ya not to ask about grades. Aw, I'm just messing with you. I am your on-wing, and that means that I am your parents, girlfriend, and drill sergeant all rolled up into one. Don't tell Marwinn as he might get jealous. You can pretty much tell or ask me anything, and I am obliged to help you. Don't ever lie to me, and we'll be just fine. The other above is for not puking. I'll have to work it in diplomatically, but that's really what it's for. I'm glad you didn't use that little blue I bag gave you in the brief. I like to hit the aerobatics hard right away to see what I have to work with. You have steel guts, congratulations.

"The last thing I'm gonna tell ya, and you don't have to write this down, is don't get discouraged. Anyone can be cogent, responsive, and gregarious when things went well at the office and you're snugglin' up with your honey after a great day. Your character is developed and truly shows itself in tough times when everything did not go as planned. That's why some soldiers and officers get silver stars, medals of valor, and such. They keep chugging under the toughest of circumstances. So stop being such a mope. Buck up, stay in the fight, and be a man. Embrace the struggle, for through it, we come to know ourselves. That will be all."

CHAPTER 12

HER IDEA

I completed the week of flying, and Marwinn and I were not assigned duty, nor flights for the weekend. We were hanging out on our polyester couches in our two-bedroom apartment at the Ashley Club just off of Scenic Highway in East Pensacola. The place was relatively new and clean. It had a gym and a pool. This was a huge upgrade over our last rental in Colorado, a rundown house we referred to as "The Brig," the Navy term for jail. We were sipping Bud Lights and just chilling on Friday evening.

Mark was ahead of me in flight training, thanks to my three weeks of office duty and jaw healing. He was scheduled for Fam Eight on Monday, and I would be attempting Fam Four. Mark ran into a little trouble as he was "downed" on Fam Five for an inability to land safely. That meant he had to complete two practice flights and Fam Five over again in addition to three or four days of admin for the whole fiasco. He wasn't himself. He was wrought with self-doubt, mildly depressed, and irritable.

I remember the weird grading system. There were about fifteen categories for each flight. They were such events as ground ops, air work, spins, speed and configuration changes, takeoffs, and landings. One could earn a grade of below average, above average, average, or unsatisfactory for each of these. Any unsat would mean you were down until re-educated and approved to return to the syllabus. An unsat was also considered two below averages, so your overall grade point average took a hit to boot. I was surprised by Mark getting a down so quickly. It seemed unfair to expect proficiency in only the fifth flight of his life. Mark, like me, had no previous flight time nor training. We commiserated and decided that his ex on-wing instructor was a hard-headed anus. Ex because, out of fairness, a SNA would no longer be assigned to fly with an instructor who downed him or her.

I suggested we get out and do something to forget about flying for a minute and maybe ease some of our pain. Mark had taken Jolene—yes, the one from the gas station—out to dinner twice, and she said she wanted to rent a boat and cruise around the bays sometime. I asked Marwinn to give her a call and find out more about it. He spoke with Jolene, and she concocted the plan.

We were to meet her and one of her friends tomorrow morning at the Avalon Bay Marina by the Highway 10 bridge, about ten miles southwest of Milton, at 0900. There was a huge billboard advertising rentals that no one could miss that we all saw twice a day on our commutes to and from Milton Naval Air Station. Jolene said we should get there early to have a better chance at renting a boat on a Saturday. She would bring food and beer, and we would spring for the boat.

I asked Marwinn, "What's her friend's name and how much does she weigh? I guess I could take one for the team and entertain the hefty one. Does she have any teeth? How many coolers of food does she require? I wonder how big a boat we should get?"

Mark admonished, "Hey, maybe stop being such a judgmental dickhead, and you might actually like Jilly Ree. Maybe she's model material, ya know, like a Southern belle or whatever is viewed as beautiful in this hellhole."

I replied not without sarcasm, "Oh yeah, I'm sure Jilly REEEE looks just like Daisy Duke."

Ironically, Jolene did.

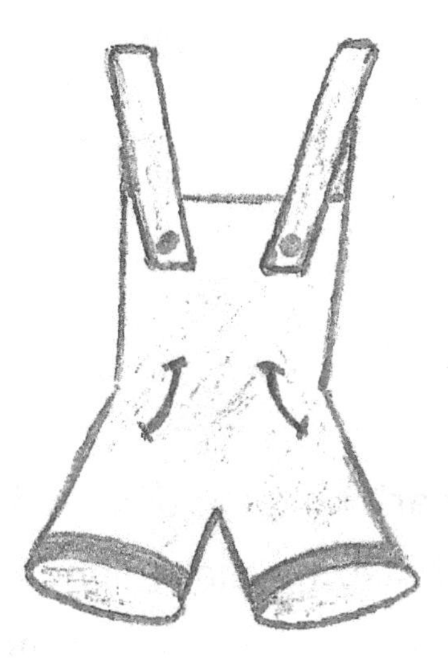

CHAPTER 13

OVERALLS

I continued to daydream. I was rubbing my face and considering a shave. *Nah, no shave required for this baby face,* I thought as I recalled the day I met Jill Marie.

We reported as ordered at 0830 to the Avalon Bay Marina. We noticed that there were no vessels at the pier with the Fishing Boats sign. There were, however, a few decent-looking runabouts with walk-through windshields and 175 horsepower Evinrude outboard engines on them at the pier to our left. We went inside the shack at the crux of the T-shaped pier and arranged to rent one of the nineteen-foot Bayliner pleasure boats for $150 for the day.

We hit the "head," a Navy term for bathroom, locked the car, and loaded our gear onto boat number five. We returned to the parking lot and waited near Marwinn's convertible red Mustang that Jolene so much adored. It was now 0900 and a wave of paranoia hit me. I was sure it was a setup and Billy Ray, Ed Earl, and a slew of their redneck buddies would soon be there to give us the what for and take good care of us.

I then thought that what if Marwinn was right and Jilly actually showed up and was some sort of prima donna babe. How could she possibly have any interest in Scarface, my new nickname.

Marwinn said, "Heads up, incoming!" as a football was making its way through the air toward my torso.

We played catch. I was grateful for the diversion, and again Marwinn had rescued me from myself.

The girls rolled up in a newer, metallic, light maroon Chevy Celebrity, apparently Jilly's car. Jolene got out wearing her signature cutoffs, tank top, and flip-flops. Her hair was pulled back into a neat ponytail, and she was wearing black-rimmed, oversized sunglasses and a light blue ball cap. She ran up to Marwinn and gave him a hug and peck on the cheek. Mark gave her a bear hug, picked her up, and gave her a half spin. They were all smiles. Marwinn tried to give her some grief by pointing to his wrist. It was now 0920.

She teasingly said, "It's a woman's prerogative to be socially late. Especially when she wants a man to build up an appetite for her. And besides, it allows a girl to make an entrance."

I thought, *Appetite, huh, more like a crippling anxiety*. But make an entrance Jilly Ree did.

She walked up smartly with an off-white canvas beach bag slung over her shoulder. She told us that the cooler was in the already-open trunk of her car. She told Jolene to stop playing kissy face and to grab her crap. She stood there impatiently as I picked up the cooler and Jolene retrieved her royal blue nylon backpack. Marwinn shut the trunk, and Jolene bumped the car door closed with her butt. Jilly clicked her key fob twice, and the car acknowledged with two short honks.

She said, "Hi, I'm Jill, where's the boat?"

Jolene pointed. "Over there." Then her face slackened

when she saw the empty fishing pier. "There aren't any boats. What happened? I told you to get here early."

"Ours is number five right over there," Mark quickly offered as he always aimed to fix things fast.

Jolene whispered, "A fancy boat, cool," and she looked at Marwinn in disbelief.

"Ahoy, ladies, to the boat," he offered with an encouraging smirk and overhead wave of his right arm.

He took Jolene's bag, I lugged the cooler, and we started toward the boat.

Jill's body matched her personality. Militant, utilitarian, and firm. She had a clean jawline and a strong, thin neck topped with a pretty but no-nonsense face underneath gold wire Ray-Ban sunglasses and long, flowing, dark brunette, almost black hair. A white Adidas cycling cap sat atop her head. The muscles of her arms and legs flexed as she purposefully strutted down the pier. I noticed her lightly tanned skin. She wore a matching clean white T-shirt and bright white ankle socks and brand-new super white Adidas cross trainers adorned her feet. Her five-foot, four-inch, 120-pound frame surely possessed a six-pack stomach underneath her clean and neat blue jean Oshkosh B'Gosh overall shorts.

"Wow," I whispered and I purposefully closed my accidentally agape mouth.

We boated around Escambia and Pensacola Bays on a beautiful Saturday in mid-July. We drifted a while, listened to music on the "dee lux" stereo as Jolene called it, and ate PB and J and ham and cheese sandwiches. We had chips, cookies, and beer for dessert. We saw the gorgeous bright blue F-18s of the Blue Angels take off from Pensacola Naval Air Station. All seven of them were no doubt heading out for a weekend air show. It was awesome. Two of them roared up and down the beach a few times as they waited for the rest of the team to launch. They delighted our party, the beachgoers, and the throng of other boats around us.

We anchored on a sandbar and swam and played catch with a Frisbee and the football. I saw Jilly wiggle out of her overalls as she revealed the rest of her svelte build wrapped in a both conservative and provocative royal-blue Body Glove two-piece swimsuit that I had seen triathletes wear. I tried not to stare, but I found her captivating. She caught me looking more than once. She was a woman of few words, and I was too intimidated by her looks, physique, and confidence to talk.

Mark and Jolene in her pink bikini were still frolicking in the surf when Jilly and I returned to the boat. We toweled dry and I got us each a bottle of water. We sat across from one another on the bow of the boat, just casually lounging with our crossed legs stretched out in front of us.

She broke the ice by saying, "So apparently you're not a Blue Angel and you're not fighting at a gas station right now, so what is it exactly that you guys do?" I looked at her dumbfounded and then she smiled and said, "Please forgive me for not knowing, but my mom told me to steer clear of you Navy boys, and I pretty much have."

I was still molten from her smile, but I managed to speak.

"We are in flight training. We are learning how to fly T-34s, the Navy's initial airplane for beginners. I hope to someday get Navy wings and fly jets." I felt like a nerdy second grader struggling to give any right answer.

"Well, tell Richard Gere, Tom Cruise, and shucks, Lou Gossett's grandma I said hello, should you see them around jet school campus," she responded. "My family moved to Milton from Chicago after my dad went on strike from United Airlines as an airplane mechanic. He heard there was steady work here for mechanics with General Dynamics, who has Navy contracts to fix airplanes. So I met Jolene in my new neighborhood, and we became childhood friends. She's a great person even though she talks funny. By the way, I go by Jill. She's the only one that gets away with this Jilly Ree nonsense. She found out that my middle name is Marie, and that was all she needed to start teasing me with my new Southern nickname, assigned by her. I tackled her over it when we were ten, and we started laughing, so now I guess it's just something stupid that bonds us. So please just call me Jill. Jolene sure likes Mark, probably because he punched out her loser old boyfriend. So how did you guys meet?"

I told her we roomed together in college and about Navy ROTC, and that was how we wound up in Pensacola. I told her that we had something in common as my dad was a United mechanic and that I, too, grew up near Chicago, but that we stayed and my family just gutted out the airline strikes. I started to relax and not feel like such a dolt. She put me at ease. She was inquisitive yet considerate.

She thought it was cool that I left home for college in Colorado and now lived in another new place. She said that she finally got her own apartment in P-Cola and that she still wanted to move on. She wanted to travel out West, maybe to California or even Alaska. She earned her nursing degree from Pensacola Junior College and was now working in the emergency room at the community hospital. She said she would never be a true Southerner and that she just saw "too much pain and stupidity in Florida" and wanted to geographically distance herself from it. I thought but didn't say stupidity might run rampant in other places too. I think it was Ralph Waldo Emerson who said traveling is a fool's paradise? Yep, probably Wally.

Mark and Jolene climbed back in the boat. The afternoon flew by, and we had to gas up and return the small runabout by 1700. Mark barked, "Man and hoist the forward anchor, ya scar-faced, starry-eyed swabby!" in his best pirate voice.

I replied, "Aye, sir, ya land-lubbin', order-givin' ass pain." I then hauled in the line and stowed the anchor in its forward compartment.

The wind and waves whipped up a bit, and we had a

fun roller-coaster-type ride back to the marina. Jolene and Jill bobbed up and down, bending their knees, and whooped, woohoo'd, and giggled until we got into smooth water inside the no-wake buoys near the pier. Mark and I took turns driving and just had some fun cutting water cookies and making figure eights, much to the girls' delight.

We returned the boat and got dressed on the dock. I pretended to be looking forward, but my eyes, hidden underneath sunglasses, were cocked to the left as I sneakily and probably sinfully watched Jilly Ree adorn herself with those intriguing overall shorts.

We walked to the cars. We said our goodbyes. I asked Jill how she liked the boat.

She replied, "Thanks. It was awesome, really fun, especially when I wasn't being ogled."

I was a little put off, as I had just sprung for half of the price of the rental boat and gas and agreed to the blind date, and I wasn't expecting her snarky response.

Irritated, I asked if she was being sincere or sarcastic.

Teasingly, she said, "Mmmmm, you decide." She added, "But I was definitely sincere when I said I see too much pain."

Then she kissed her right index finger and touched it to the scar on the left side of my jaw.

As she walked away, she looked back and lowered her sunglasses in a provocative manner and batted her brownish green eyes. She smiled a sly grin exposing bright white, seemingly perfect teeth. Now sure that I was watching, she turned and wiggled her butt, and I was treated to a teeter-totter tilting of those damned overalls.

CHAPTER 14

INTERPRETATION

Mark told the guys about our day of boating with Jolene and Jilly Ree. They had a field day with me. They taunted me and amused themselves commenting on Jill's antics and remarks.

Farts McSorley intimated, "Dude, she must be way into you to wiggle her butt for you. On second thought, maybe she was saying, kiss this fine ass goodbye!"

Everyone laughed except me.

I was trying to get back at him and said, "Thanks,

Gary. I truly value the opinion of the guy we call Farts. How did you earn that nickname anyway? Did you crack one off at the wrong time? Did you rip a loud and damp one at a wedding, funeral, or in church?"

"Naw, I got it for the sounds my OP flip-flops make when they're wet, squishing, squeaking, and making suction noises under my feet. Anyway, there is a pretty good chance she likes you after that rad and righteous boating trip. Next time take me and I'll try some wake surfing," he added with his "heeyah" kind of chuckle.

He was easing off a bit, and I appreciated it.

He then told me that his nickname started in high school. He said he was reading a book by Ray Bradbury in which one of the characters simply said that people must be amused, and that's the way he looks at it.

He continued, "Let people be happy and think what they want. They, not knowing that I pretty much got straight A's in Biochem in college. I like to surf, and my easygoing persona plays well with the ladies. Like Bill said, all the world's a stage, and we are merely the players. I choose to amuse and play the fool."

Shocked and impressed by his apparent wealth of

knowledge, I simply said, "I will never call you Farts again."

He responded, "Don't sweat it, Ruddster. I've made my peace with it."

I harbored a secret jealousy, having yet to find any personal peace in my life.

CHAPTER 15

SOLO

I hung up the small blue face towel and noticed that the hook to the right of the sink was wobbly. I made a mental note to tighten that up later.

I passed the much feared and dreaded Fam Thirteen check.

In the Familiarization stage a student pilot learns the basics of flying along with a litany of emergency procedures, just in case anything unusual happens. I learned to take off, land, and spin the airplane. The spin was a nose-high controlled stall with full rear stick and then full rudder to the side of the spin that resulted in a nose-low continuous turn until the pilot flew his or her way out of it. The spins were fun. I also learned to glide the airplane to a safe landing area, usually a farm field, in the event of an engine failure. These training events were called HAPLs and LAPLs for the corresponding high or low altitude power loss. We didn't actually land in the field as the instructor would take the airplane around four hundred feet of altitude and knock off training once the aircraft was in a safe position to land.

The thirteenth flight was the safe to solo check ride. My check instructor, Marine Corps Captain "Downs" Wantrowski or the "Polish Terror" as the students referred to him, was surprisingly quiet and matter-of-fact. He asked a few emergency procedures in the brief, which was standard, and I spit them out as I had many times before. He then just quietly observed that I could accomplish the maneuvers and touch and go landings. He said in the debrief that many students can fly just fine, but that they get lost and can't make their way back to our home field in accordance with the course rules. He said he was happy that I didn't get lost and gave me an above averages for headwork and navigation.

I, of course, heaped a ton of anxiety upon myself prior to my first check ride ever in an airplane. I still feel a bit anxious to this day on even the most routine checks or observation rides. At least it keeps me in the books.

I flew by myself for the first time out of North Whiting Field in Milton, Florida, on Tuesday, July 25th, 1989. On Fam Fourteen, the last flight of the stage, I flew to Saufley Field, an outlying navy airstrip, and did the required five touch and go landings. I then flew up into a training block between five and nine thousand feet and turned and went up and down and spun once. The hop was only slotted for ninety minutes, so before long, I had to follow the course rules back to base.

While I don't think I broke surly bonds nor touched God's face, I enjoyed the solace of solo flight. Like a little kid, I felt reassured that I could do it all by myself. I realized that I actually enjoyed flying and I was grateful for my newfound remedial confidence in myself as a pilot.

Maybe I found a little bit of the peace that Smarts was talking about.

CHAPTER 16

PRECISION

Having safely soloed, I started in on the next phase of flight training, Precision Aerobatics. I learned how to execute the wingover, barrel, and aileron rolls, half and full Cuban eights, inverted flight, split S, Immelmann reversals, and the vertical loop. I loved it. The training came hard and fast. It was only a five-flight phase, with two of the five being solos. I aced the one-day class and received excellent flight grades as I was not a puker.

We were also introduced to aircraft carrier landings

during this phase. We flew to landings cued by an optical device at the side of the runway. It was called the meatball for its spherical reddish orange glow when properly aligned to precisely hit the targeted spot on the deck. Pretty cool.

I concentrated on flying and mostly kept Jill Marie out of my mind.

Marwinn had not been himself and was having trouble with Jolene. She wanted time he didn't have as he was busy flying and standing various watches. She'd get particularly peeved when he couldn't see her on weekends. He was having night terrors to boot and was having trouble sleeping. I found him once at three in the morning making a raucous clatter. He was showering while sleeping. He was wobbling and babbling that he had to get to work as he was late for his flight brief. I managed to wake him up and get him back in bed.

Smarts McSorley, unfortunately, was a puker. He was miserable throughout the aerobatic phase and mostly flew straight and level on his solos. I felt bad for him, but I admired his gumption. He made it through PAs.

Harry and Petey were well adjusted and getting great grades. Petey was shorter than the rest of us, about five foot, six inches tall. He looked like a cross between Columbo and Joe Pesci. He didn't mind. Nothing seemed to bother either of them.

I, on the other hand, was bothered plenty. The temporary tooth installed by the new Navy dentist fell out. I now only had the weird-feeling metal bracket/bridge in my jaw. The dentist said he would leave it there until my permanent fake tooth arrived from the lab. He said it would keep the rear molar and whatever other tooth it was attached to from collapsing inward. What fun.

So with problems abounding and the stress of flight school itself piling up upon us, I thought it prudent not to whine or inquire about Jill. I stuffed thoughts of her way down into my being and rationalized the situation to just another something that I don't understand. I added women, specifically one woman, to my list of quantum physics, electricity, and nuclear power. She was still there though, nagging me from the bottom of my feet, up my spinal cord, and into the base of my brain. My feelings of inadequacy and insecurity were transferred from flying to the most intriguing woman I had ever met.

My mind taunted, "Call her, get her number from

Jolene, don't call her, she hates you flyboys, be a man and invite her to dinner, ask her about her interests, don't be such a wuss..."

I was racked with uncertainty and hid in my job. I was a wuss, precisely.

CHAPTER 17

COURT DATE

"All rise. The Honorable Judge Thomas J. Kelly will now preside over First Judicial Circuit Court of Florida in the Milton, Florida County Courthouse. Court is now in session," said Bailiff Daniel Catello in a perfectly respectful, monotone voice.

The tall, middle-aged judge with circular gold wire-framed glasses walked in from behind his massive desk, paused, and momentarily stood at attention while surveying the large crowd before him. He then took a deep breath, smoothed his black robe, which was draped over a clean white collar and neatly knotted navy blue tie, and sat down in the reddish mahogany leather chair behind his bench.

He started, "Be seated, please, ladies and gentlemen. Now, the cases before me this morning have many elements and are apt for sensationalism. I will not allow cameras nor videotaping of the proceedings. You may take written notes discreetly, but you are not to read, talk, nor conduct any personal business while seated in this courtroom."

Right on cue, Bailiff Catello tapped a newspaper of a man three rows back. He folded it up and started to pay attention.

His Honor continued, "I will not tolerate outbursts nor grandstanding of any kind. So long as you all understand and behave in quiet and courteous fashion, we will proceed. Please don't force my hand and require someone to leave the room or, worse, be charged with contempt at any time during these proceedings. I truly appreciate your cooperation on this splendidly sultry mid-August day. Please understand that this is quite a large crowd in attendance, and our air conditioners are doing their best in this aging but historic building."

Quite a large crowd, huh? Boy howdy, I thought. Who knew that getting kicked in the jaw could be such a kick in the head. I sat at the front right of the crowd on the plaintiff side without representation. Mark Marwinn was, surprisingly, the defendant to my left. Mark had a lawyer next to him. Why? We were dressed in short-sleeved tropical white uniforms with black shoulder boards that had one gold stripe and star indicating our rank of ensign. Some call these "ice cream suits" as they are similar to what the Good Humor man wears. Our nifty white hats with black visors and the Navy's silver and gold emblem sat on tables in front of us. LTCOL Collens, Capt. Franklin, Deputy Sheriff Walsh, Jed Gallishaw, Jolene, Jill, reporters, and dozens of assorted locals were in attendance.

The judge nodded at the clerk, who said, "The State of Florida versus Mark Michael Marwinn, case number 89 C.R. 102."

Judge Kelly kept going. "Now, I have met in chambers with the officials and lawyers involved in this case. It is my understanding that you, Ensign Marwinn, physically assaulted one William Ray Johnson and one

Edward Earl Hadley approximately eight weeks ago at a gas station owned by a Mr. Jed Gallishaw in Milton. Is that correct?"

Mark stood and said, "Yes, sir."

"Furthermore you are being charged with the misdemeanor offense of disorderly conduct resulting in public unrest. Do you understand these charges?

Mark's response: "Yes, Your Honor."

"How do you plea?"

"Not guilty."

I was miffed and disturbed. I could barely keep up with the proceedings. I thought I was going to court to testify against Billy Ray, not press charges, and put this whole mess behind us. Now Mark was on trial, with a lawyer and completely unbeknownst to me? What the fudge! He didn't tell *me*?

Judge Kelly addressed me. "Apparently Ensign Marwinn's actions at the gas station on this day were in your defense. Is that correct, Ensign Rudd?"

I stood and responded, "Yes, sir, to the best of my knowledge. I was not conscious at the time. I am grateful for his help..."

"That's enough," the judge interrupted.

He then asked Mark why he acted in an overtly violent manner.

Mark explained, "I came out of the small store..."

"What did you buy?" asked the judge.

"Beer," and as Mark continued, a Bible Belt gasp came from the gallery, "and two bottles of water and gas for the car. I then saw Ensign Rudd laying on the ground and a tall, thin man muttering angry words, scowling, and getting ready to kick him in the head or face."

There was a greater gasp.

"Maintain decorum," Judge Kelly politely warned.

"So I grabbed this unknown guy and slammed him into the gas pump. He was flailing and trying to fight back, so I punched him. Then his buddy tried to jump me, so I ducked and kneed him in the stomach as he passed me. With the assailants subdued, I stopped and they fled. We waited for an ambulance and the police, my apologies, the deputy sheriff."

The judge then asked Mark's counsel for his input. The handsome lawyer dressed in a fashionably sharp, dark blue suit and a Brooks Brothers red silk power tie recapped the incident. It seemed as though I had heard or told this same story a thousand times. He indicated that Billy Ray started the physical part of the altercation and that Mark would not have otherwise been involved. He also stated that Mark and I had no prior legal records nor convictions against us and that we had no interest in fighting anyone that day. He furthermore said that the fight was two against one and not in Mark's favor. He ended with the fact that Mark's actions may have very well saved my life as the nickel-toed weapon had already punched one hole in my head, and I likely would have received at least one more had it not been for Ensign Marwinn's actions. He stated that Mark acted in justifiable self-defense and with appropriate force. He asked that the charges against Mark be rescinded without prejudice.

I was impressed with the young, talented Jeffrey Gilbert, Attorney at Law. I wanted to rant in Mark's defense. I was angry at a legal system that was trying the wrong man, and looking back, I was mostly hurt that Mark didn't tell me about his culpability and that he himself was still on the hook for this fiasco. Gilbert's eloquence and ability to intertwine legal facts and information made a much better statement for Mark than I could have possibly mustered from my legally ignorant and overly emotional mind.

His Honor asked if restitution had been made for the broken gas pump mentioned in the sheriff's report. The lawyer responded that his client, Mark, paid the gas station owner $189.75 for the pump repair as indicated by the cancelled check submitted to the court as evidence of goodwill on his client's behalf.

Judge Kelly said that he found Marwinn's actions "reasonable under extremis." He then ruled in Mark's favor and declared him not guilty of the charge brought against him. The charge was dismissed and Mark would retain his clean record.

Jolene started clapping quickly and incessantly. Everyone, including the judge, looked over at her, and she whispered "Sorry" as a tear rolled down her cheek. Jilly Ree gave her there, there now pats on the back, and there were a few chuckles and then order restored itself.

The judge told Mark and his counsel they were free to go and asked the clerk to move on to the next case.

Mark went and sat in the back of the courtroom, and the clerk announced, "The State of Florida versus

William Ray Johnson, case number 89 C.R. 103."

With that, Billy Ray appeared wearing a bright orange jumpsuit and was seated on the left side of the crowd at the defendant's table. He was joined there by a tired slob in a cheap tan polyester suit with a brown mustard-stained tie and a nicely dressed plain Jane in a dark gray skirt suit with a clean white oxford shirt. Billy sat with his head down and looked to be brooding.

"Mr. Johnson," the judge started, "you are charged with the misdemeanors of disorderly conduct, fleeing the scene of a known crime, resisting arrest, and attempted battery of an officer of the law during your arrest. Do you understand these charges?"

There was only a nod and a smirk from Billy. The public defender stood and said, "We do, Your Honor, and plead not guilty to all charges," but it was too late. The judge was annoyed.

The judge then asked me if I recognized the individual dressed in orange and if he was in fact the individual who struck me on the day in question. I stood and respectfully confirmed that it was Billy who kicked me, using the filthy boot that was bagged as evidence and rested on yet another table in front of me. I also stated that I did not seek restitution nor wish to bring any charges against him.

Billy glanced at me and smiled, as though he won. He turned a little more to his right to see the crowd and noticed Jolene and Jill sitting not behind him, but on the side of the plaintiff. His smile vanished and his face flushed into a sweaty red glow.

The judge accepted the not guilty plea and listened to an argument from the defending attorney that my comments about Jolene and insult to Billy's tooth were taunts and that consideration and leniency should be granted to his client. Plain Jane also asked for less jail time and credit for time served by Billy Ray.

Judge Thomas Kelly became stern and most serious.

His remarks:

"First, thank you, Ms. Madeline LeClair, for your attendance this morning and for your explanation of the terms of Mr. Johnson's probation due to his previous convictions. Your efforts on behalf of your clients, the county, and the state are tireless and most commendable."

The slender thirty-something probation officer with auburn hair pulled straight back into a neat bun stood and nodded her head with a slight bow and demure smile.

"However, Mr. Johnson, I am in no way pleased to have you as a defendant in my courtroom again. Your continued criminal, physically abusive, and hot-headed behavior has landed you in jail, and you will receive credit for your time served. You will stand when addressed in this court of law!"

Billy slowly and reluctantly joined his representation in their upright postures.

"You will continue to be incarcerated for the full ninety-day penalty for your clear and willful violation of the terms of your probation. I find you guilty of the charges brought against you today, and you are hereby fined one thousand five hundred dollars payable to this court. Although Ensign Rudd will not bring charges against you, the State of Florida may. In lieu of the testimony and statements given by two naval officers, a deputy sheriff, and two eyewitnesses at the scene, you will be required to attend a preliminary hearing and possibly be arraigned for felonious criminal assault. Your bond for this hearing is set at ten thousand dollars. I have heard from your attorney and probation officer. Do you have anything to say for yourself, Mr. Johnson."

Billy Ray Johnson went nuts. He said that everything was rigged against him and that he should have been allowed to change clothes and look better.

He ranted, "I can't pay no fifteen hunnert bucks and I ain't workin' for no slave wages in some crappy work program neither."

He said that if I just kept my mouth shut, he wouldn't have had to shut it for me. His anger grew and his eyes were scary wide open when he turned and danced a little hobo jig for the audience. He smiled broadly, exposing his grimy, tobacco-stained, crooked teeth.

"Here's something to look at," he yelled. "You came for entertainment, well, you got it! Hell, I'm better than a circus monkey. Weeeeeee!"

He was shuffling his feet and waving his arms over his head.

The front row of the gallery, just behind a lovely oak rail, leaned back in their chairs, scared. Others in the audience pointed and clamored. Ms. LeClair and his lawyer backed away from Billy Ray. I dropped my jaw, then clenched it, expecting another attack.

He was now making hissing sounds and clawing at the air toward the crowd.

Judge Kelly banged his gavel at least a dozen times as Billy Ray lost his junk. He ordered, "Apprehend and cuff this dancing lunatic!"

Deputy Sheriff Walsh and the bailiff restrained Billy and slammed him facedown on the oak table. They cuffed his hands behind his back. He was hauled off while muttering, "Cop, pig, bastards" and apparently trying to throw sweat on anyone near him by quickly twisting his head and flipping his long, scraggly, wet brown hair at them.

Three hard, loud bangs resounded through the courtroom. The dank air went dead silent.

The judge calmly said, "I will have order. Now, everyone, please be seated."

This was literally not his first rodeo. He matter-of-factly directed the clerk to note that William Ray Johnson was now being held in contempt of court, that he would have to answer for his actions, and that he would also be restrained for all future legal appearances.

Judge Thomas J. Kelly gently tapped the square oak block on his desk with his gavel and politely said, "This court is adjourned."

As I left, I noted that the bench, the witness box, the rail, and most of the wood around me was aged, light brown oak. I was in a sea of oak. Huge oak trees started as small acorns. Gigantic, gargantuan growth, Gee.

CHAPTER 18

A DATE

I caught up to Mark and the girls in the parking lot. Before I could start my interrogation, Mark suggested we get some food. He was an expert at smoothing things over and he used nutrition as one of his tools.

We were seated at a diner near the Avalon Marina as Mark and I were still banned from Milton proper. Mark explained that he received the summons from Deputy Walsh as a matter of procedure. He said that Walsh's boss gets upset when no tickets are issued because that's how the county generates revenue to pay their sorry asses. Hence, someone had to get one, and he was the only participant there, so he won the door prize. Walsh said not to worry, it would all get settled later. Taking no chances and fearing for his livelihood as both a pilot and an officer, Mark hired the attorney as insurance, just in case some hick judge hated him, the military, non-locals, and for all other biases that might be brought against him. Jolene and Mark withheld the information from me as they thought it best not to give me one more thing to sweat over.

It worked. Then I was hit with a wave of appreciation. I now knew that Mark took one for the team and I was grateful. I thought of his night terrors and figured that the court date must have in part been the cause. In a daydream trance, I contemplated the word "friendship."

Maybe it means sacrifice?

The triumvirate woke me up, and I ordered steak and eggs, my standard brunch. I thanked Jill for wearing white and supporting my team. She was dressed in a mid-thigh length, tastefully gorgeous, pristine white Ralph Lauren tennis dress.

She quipped, "I wasn't there for you idiots. I was there to support my best friend."

Jolene flashed a beaming smile, exposing her beautiful white teeth.

We ate quietly and struggled for conversation. We talked a little about our day of boating. We briefly mentioned Billy Ray and how we all hoped we had seen the last of him.

Jill and Mark started talking about Jolene and how she should go to college.

Jolene shut them down and said, "One, I'm not that smart. Two, I don't have money for tuition. And three, how about we talk about happy things, damn it?"

After a bout of my standard mental torture, I asked Jill out to dinner on Saturday night.

She slowly teased, "Hmmm, let me see…you know…I do like to eat…and I usually eat dinner in the evening… but I am working nights…but I am off this weekend… but I have to walk Bailey, my dog…and Jolene and I might get tattoos…"

We were all hanging on her every word.

Jolene elbowed her and said, "Very cute, now answer the man! And, Mark and I can't come because we're…

um...seeing a movie."

With casual conviction Jill finally said, "Okay, it's a date. Pick me up at 1800; that's military time for 6:00 p.m. We'll walk my dog first and then you can show me the best night on the town ever!"

At first I was relieved and excited that I actually asked her out and she said yes. Then my perpetual anxiety and self-doubt kicked in. Was she serious or sarcastically messing with me again? Tough nut. *Do I need a tough nut in my life? Do I even like her? Shut up, Tom, and just take this brunette, athletic, and no-nonsense babe on a hopefully pleasant date.*

CHAPTER 19

NOW WHAT?

Now let me think. I was staring down at the rather clean commode. The court appearance was on a Wednesday, and I had Thursday off. I remember because it was unusual to get a weekday off. I used the time to work out and study for the basic instrument phase of training. I looked in the mirror again, but now with a vacant stare. I rubbed some Old Spice stick deodorant in each armpit and wondered if I had any clean white T-shirts.

So it must have been a Friday that I flew BI-1, the first flight of five for this segment of instruction. BIs were weird. The flight student sat in the back seat of the airplane for these and had a cloth, antique white cotton hood pulled over his or her head so the flying could only be accomplished via the instrument clusters on the gray metal panel in front of the control stick. These hops could be flown at night, and sometimes the instructor would forego the "under the bag" requirement as one couldn't see much from the back seat at night. The maneuvers were basic but challenging. We practiced controlling heading, altitude, and airspeed while straight and level, and while turning, climbing, and descending. We also sped up, slowed down, and lowered and raised the flaps and landing gear. Of course strict procedures were required and memorized for each maneuver, and they were accomplished by flying S1, level speed change, alpha, bravo, and charlie patterns, et cetera and ad nauseam.

I tried to develop my own instrument scan by continuously returning to the altitude gyro after each individual check of the altimeter, airspeed indicator, slip and skid indicator, engine power gauge, and others. I wasn't good at it. Sometimes an instructor would start banging on the canopy. I would ask about the noise over the inter phone.

He would then explain that it was just the ball trying to get back in the airplane. The "ball" was the slip and skid indicator and was integral to balanced flight. We tried to keep it in the middle of a slightly arched fluid tube on the instrument panel, similar to that of a carpenter's level.

I liked to fly fast, look outside, and pull G's. This instrument stuff made me impatient and left me frustrated.

We heard a "Mayday, Mayday, eh...Mayday!" call on our guard frequency. Guard was and still is an emergency frequency that we monitor throughout all military and civilian flights. My instructor told me to disregard it and turn my radio volume down and complete the hop. We were about done anyway. The flight instructor then took the controls and asked me to stow the bag, turn up my volume, and help him look outside for anything unusual like smoke or parachutes. We saw only clear skies. We flew around for an extra half hour or so and then returned to base with minimum fuel.

Luckily, my instructor accomplished the takeoff and landing and demoed each pattern in BI-1, so I only actually flew for maybe twenty or thirty minutes. In the debrief he told me that horseshit was normal for this flight, and that I should just keep plugging and I would get better. He said he knew it wasn't really fun flying, but you just had to push through and persevere. He graded me out at straight average and I was grateful. I was all over the sky.

I was walking outside of flight ops after the BI-1 debrief when Petey, my college buddy, intercepted me. He was dressed in khakis and was apparently the student squadron duty officer of the day. He told me to stow my gear and to go see Snake in his office ASAFP. Now what? I asked what was going on, but Petey was sworn to secrecy and wouldn't budge. He looked serious and a little frightened. I was hoping he was toying with me, but somehow I knew better.

I reported as ordered and stood at attention in my sweaty green flight suit. I was alone this time, in front of LTCOL Collens, who was seated in his leather chair behind his desk.

He began, "At ease, Ensign Rudd, and please be

seated. I called you in today for three reasons. First, congratulations on the resolution of your legal situation. We managed to mitigate the repercussions, and the press took our side and offered a pro military slant to their articles. So, I am happy for you, Ensign Marwinn, and our squadron. I am glad that we can now put the whole situation behind us.

"Second, I have some concern about a student solo flight. Do you know why my call sign is Snake?"

I responded that I thought it was a compliment to his anatomical manhood.

He continued, "While your interpretation is probably true, because I am Black and I hope to live up to the stereotype, that is not the reason. When I was a flight student, I liked to mess with instructors and make S shapes with the airplane by cycling the rudder down the runway. I continued the ruse by feigning incompetence to new pilots in my fleet squadron by doing the 'snake' down the runway with C-130s. We scared newbies and had a ball with it. I realize that my hijinks was in direct contradiction to the safety first motto that we preach in naval aviation, but I earned myself a nickname and now I live with it.

"Now, I heard that some wise ass on a solo flight had the canopy open and was waving to his fans on the beach at an estimated altitude of five hundred feet. This aviator also interrupted the banner towing pattern along said beach and left a Piper Cub pilot scared shitless as the two aircraft flew at each other nose to nose. The Navy T-34 passed over him, and his wake ruffled the banner and threw the Cub around a bit. His buddy was flying a Decathlon and wrote down the tail number of the obvious orange and white Navy plane and called it in to our training wing. I must admit that I find this amusing, and I admire the military pilot's guts. I wish we could afford ourselves some fun every once in a while. I have the aircraft number, and I cross-referenced it with our solos for this day. Do you know anything at all about this hop, *Ensign Rudd*?"

"Yes, sir, I do" was my only possible response.

Snake looked up and to his left. "My first thought was to throw you out of the program and maybe the Navy. Maybe I could spin to the press that we wouldn't tolerate your behavior nor your legal troubles, and win local favor for the Navy and Marine Corps. I requested your training jacket. Do you know where you stand compared to your peers?"

"No, sir."

"Well, I'll tell you. You are number freaking one! You are averaging over two above average grades per hop, and your academic average is 98.6. No prior flight time. How is this possible? I want to throw you out for the benefit of the world at large, and you turn out to be some kind of Zen master prodigy pilot? I read that on PA-5, you coordinated with flight ops and the runway duty officer to avoid weather, do your aerobatics, get your landings in, and you received a two above grade for your efforts. Impressive considering over half of our flight schedule was cancelled for weather that day, and solo flights usually go ungraded. You're flying, solo nonetheless, when my instructors can't? Improbable, impossible, inconceivable.

"Are you familiar with the book character Don Quixote?"

"No, not really. Unfortunately, sir, I must admit that I am not well read."

"Well he was the Ingenious Gentleman of La Mancha, written by Miguel de Cervantes. It was written around the year 1600 and is still considered one of the greatest literary works of all time. Quixote perhaps loses his mind, becomes a knight, tries to restore chivalry and decency in the world, and fights windmills whom he supposes are archenemies. One of my takeaways is that we must choose our battles wisely or be considered a fool. I no longer snake down runways. I suggest that you take a page out of Lt. Pete Mitchell's book and start doing it safer and cleaner than everyone else.

"This now brings me to my third and most important point. Captain Franklin had long been surprising me. When I took command, I took aim at him because he was fat and I don't like fat. I flew with him. I couldn't bust him for his flying because he was better than me. Hell, he was better than everyone. He was our Instructor of the Year, but hardly poster material. So I downed him for medical reasons and told him he could come back when he was in better shape. He battled a thyroid problem all his life, but he insisted on being a Marine and a pilot. He did just that. He flew FA-18 jet fighters in the fleet but elected to instruct in T-34s by choice. He got his meds and diet in order and PT'd daily. He got himself into his best shape, and I was good to my word and let him fly again. He consistently produced our squadron's best students. He had sent twice as many students to jets than the next closest primary instructor pilot in both wings, that is all five squadrons."

"I'm sorry to interrupt, sir, but why all of the past tense?"

"Because I am told that we lost our Instructor of the Year today."

"Whoa, whoa, whoa. Are you telling me that Captain Franklin is dead?"

"Unfortunately, son, yes."

I was lost, aghast, and in disbelief. He went on to say that Franky was flying an aerobatic flight with Ensign Juanita Garcia. She bailed out and was being sent to the base hospital as we spoke. Their airplane suffered an explosion, and as of yet, Captain Franklin was unaccounted for. There was only a partial Mayday call. There was no situation, position, nor intention reported. That's all he knew. He said that he would now be my on-wing. He told me that he had the utmost respect for his lost comrade and that he would do his best for me. We were all holding on to hope for his survival, but no second parachute was observed. I was too numb to cry. He warned me not to overreact and suggested I carry on and be strong. He said that it would be a waste of God-given talent for me to give up on flying now. I would not fly on Monday, but I would meet with him at 1600 in his office. He hoped to have most of the information about Capt. Franklin's demise by then. I waded back into a world of absolute gloom, my newest personal hell. Embrace the struggle, huh?

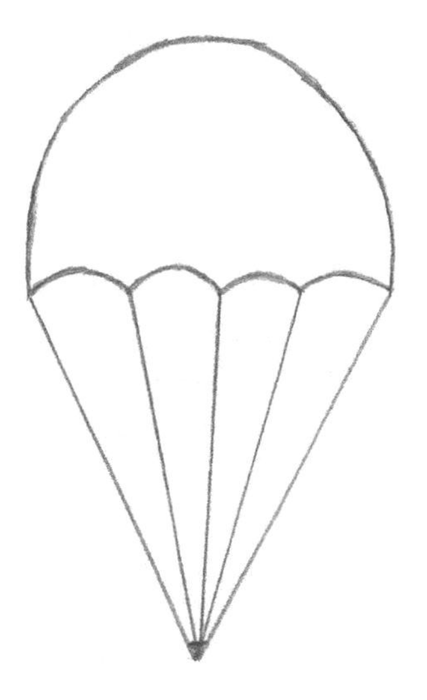

CHAPTER 20

JOHNNI

How could an airplane, specifically a T-34C, explode?

This was the question we pondered and attempted to answer. My friends were gathered in my apartment that Friday night. They knew that I liked Frankenstein and they were concerned that I might lose it. I didn't even know what it was. Maybe my mind, temper, motivation, who knows? I appreciated them being there. We chilled, sipped beer, and theorized about what may have happened.

Smarts McSorley opened with the fire triangle: fuel, oxygen, and ignition source or spark. All three are present in abundance in airplanes. There seem to be complicated fuel, oxygen, and electrical lines incongruously running everywhere in most flying machines.

Petey and Marwinn thought that maybe something broke as a result of the gravitational forces of the aerobatic flight. They both recalled "wringing it out pretty good" on all precision aero hops.

Harry Babcock provided some much-needed levity, repeatedly saying, "It just blew," from the movie *The Right Stuff*. He did add though that there was capacitor in the engine compartment that pumped high-voltage pulses out to the wing strobe lights.

McSorley added, "Yeah, dude, and an electric exciter/igniter box for engine ignition too. My on-wing showed it to me on Fam-Zero."

Petey explained that there might have been leaking high-pressure fuel being atomized with high-speed air, which would be highly combustible, even explosive.

As for me, I was too confused, numb, and sad to surmise, conjecture, or think. I did wonder though about the short Mayday call. It should have included

ISPI: Identification, Situation, Position, Intentions. All we heard was "Mayday, Mayday, Mayday," but no ISPI. Hmmm.

Not surprisingly, Smarts came up with the simple plan. He suggested that we just ask Juanita. "She's one of us, right? Wasn't she sitting by us in the auditorium when the admiral was barking at us?"

I chimed in. "He's right, I was looking down at her face-to-face when I noticed her big black nameplate, GARCIA, and how many girls named Garcia can there be? I'm going to take a shower and call it a night. I'll try to see her in the base hospital tomorrow morning. Bailouts can be gnarly. I hope she is all right. Let me go alone. Let's try not to overwhelm. Thanks, guys, and good night."

Before I headed off to bed, I raised my beer mug and offered, "To fly west is a flight we all must take for a final check ride. To Captain Ronald Franklin, United States Marine Corps."

I wondered if they were actually flying west when it happened and realized that cowboys riding off into the western sunset on horseback may well be a metaphor for death. Hmph.

"Cheers, Tommy, and here, here, Ruddster" abounded from my friends. We chinked glasses, raised them high, and knocked back hearty swigs.

The best I could muster was glum enthusiasm.

Harry added, "I heard some rumors around base that Juanita broke her arm, but that she's going to be okay."

Man, word travels fast, and now I knew why Snake summoned me so quickly. We had already learned that the partial and charred remains of Captain Franklin—still strapped to his seat and wearing his unopened parachute—had been recovered.

"Good plan, man, and good night," Petey offered in an encouraging tone.

I woke up, showered again, and brushed all of my teeth except one. I dressed in neat, clean khakis, the uniform of the day. I even put on my two award ribbons. I certainly wasn't trying to woo Ensign Juanita Garcia, but I felt like I owed her a higher level of respect. I considered the dress UOD, whites, but I thought that would be overdoing it and did not want to appear celebratory.

I made it past hospital security, assuring them that I

was not the press, and arrived at her room. It was now about 1000 and she was sitting up in her hospital bed playing with some chocolate pudding and a spoon. She was wearing a light blue gown and had a new bright white plaster cast on her right arm all the way up to her armpit. She had a swollen black left eye and a corresponding purple bruise down the side of her face. There were already flowers and balloons strewn about the room, but luckily she was alone. So maybe if I could break the ice, she would talk to me.

I knocked softly on the frame of the open door and walked into her room. I said, "Hello, Juanita," and gave her a teddy bear with a brown leather flight jacket and aviator goggles.

She said, "Um, thanks, and you are...?"

"Tom Rudd," I offered. "We made solid eye contact during the admiral's speech."

"Um, yeah, that was, um...awkward... Please call me Johnni. So, do you often visit downtrodden women whom you don't really know in hospital beds? I must look a mess," she said with southern flair.

"Uh, yeah. I know this is weird, but I *am* impressed that you find humor in your situation. I am glad to see you are in relatively good spirits. I hope your teeth are okay because that new hack Navy dentist is still working on mine." I pointed to the scar on my left cheek.

"I'm feeling good for now. We'll see when the pain meds wear off. Oh…you are one of the guys I saw in the paper. The one who lost the fight."

"Thanks for reminding me. Anyway, Captain Franklin was my on-wing, and as you read about, he helped me through some tough times. I know you have probably already told the story, but if you don't mind, could you please tell me what you think happened?"

"Oh gosh, I'm so sorry for what happened to him. He saved my life, and I so wish he could have made it out of the airplane. We were maybe midway through PA-4, the last safe-for-solo check ride. I goofed up the vertical loop and came out of the maneuver about five hundred feet too low. He demoed a good one and told me that I just needed more back stick pressure, as you know, about three G's on the back side of the loop. I overdid it. I pulled probably four or five, maybe even a momentary six G's, and we heard a loud snap, then a pop."

The crackle of fire was to come, the childish Rice Krispies side of my brain told myself.

She sighed and went on. "We both smelled the kerosene-based JP-5 jet fuel. The plane was getting squirrelly, taking max side stick and a bunch of rudder to stay upright. Capt. Franklin took the controls and started steering away from Brewton, Alabama, the small town we were near. The engine was surging, you know, like ruhhh, ruhhh, and he was struggling to control the airplane as he calmly delivered the bailout command. I blew the canopy open with the red emergency handle to my right. I disconnected my communication cords and twisted my center black buckle, releasing my harness. I crouched down on the seat, then jumped out to the right side of the plane. I was violently thrown toward the horizontal stabilizer in what seemed like slow motion. I put up my right arm and broke my humerus bone as my arm and helmet impacted the horizontal stab. My visor broke, and the left side of my face felt hot. I flailed and tumbled away from the aircraft and looked up at my chute opening as the plane blew up. Weird that I first thought, *So that's why we check that the parachute lanyard is connected on preflight.* It's the rip cord. Then I looked for another chute, but saw none. I saw burning wreckage falling to the ground in chunks. It looks cool in movies, but sickening in real life. I smelled fuel again and realized that my flight suit was wet with it. I told myself that he must have got out and I just couldn't see him through the falling debris. I was wrong. I hit the ground hard and in a daze. I just lay there wondering if my arm would ever work again and if I could get a call out on my PRC 90 radio. A farmer scooped me up. I passed out and I woke up in an ambulance."

Sounds familiar, I thought.

A tear welled then fell from her damaged left eye, and I felt bad for making her relive her nightmare.

I reached out to take her hand. She willingly gripped it with force. I thanked her for confirming what I already knew. I knew that my mentor and now new hero acted with honor, valor, and cool integrity in the face of tremendous adversity. He sacrificed himself for another and probably more folks on the ground. I, too, wished he had just a little more time to jump out of the killing machine.

We held hands quietly for some time, probably five minutes. I broke our silence. I said that most guys call me Ruddster because the child of a friend pointed at me and called me that. "Why do you call yourself Johnni when Juanita is such a pretty name?"

She told me that it is better than Consuelo, the mean and degrading insult that was shouted at her by rude boys because she was Hispanic and always short for her age. I wasn't expecting her honest, ribald joke, and I let out a subdued chuckle. She giggled then winced, let go of my hand, and cupped the side of her face. She figured that this aviation dream of hers was and is dominated by males, and she liked the ring of Johnni Garcia, so she chose her own tomboyish nickname, started introducing herself as Johnni, and it worked.

Was everyone smarter than I was?

She said, "Thanks for coming and don't be a such a creepy stranger" with a warm smile. I was awed by a great example of yet another quality human being. She truly had my sincerest admiration of her humility, bravery, and intelligence.

I left just in time. My tears were well on their way out of their ducts and onto my appreciative face.

I then realized that I needed to pull myself together, buy some flowers, and get ready for my date with Jill that night.

CHAPTER 21

THE TOWN

We gave Bailey a long walk and tucked the smallish, yellow, friendly, and adorable Labrador mix in her bed with a treat in Jill's cozy apartment.

"Bailey really likes you, Tom. Thanks for the walk and the flowers; now where to?" Jill asked as I opened the front passenger door of my Jeep Cherokee.

"Well, you said you wanted a night on the town, so here we go," I responded with raised eyebrows and a hopeful smile.

We started at the Sandshaker on Pensacola Beach. It looked kind of like an open-air shed, nothing too special. The establishment is famous for their frozen, chocolatey Bushwacker rum drinks. I ordered two in cheesy plastic souvenir mugs, and we sipped the refreshing quaffs through purple straws and walked the lovely white sand beach toward the elegant Flounder's restaurant. I told her not to get too excited as I had a different place planned for dinner tonight. She said she'd like try Flounder's some time as she heard it was great, and though she wasn't a fan of seafood, she would probably enjoy the ambiance.

We saw a school of mullet swimming along the shore. She explained about the Mullet Toss at the Flora-Bama biker tavern on the Florida/Alabama state line. Florida supporters throw dead mullets in a contest to see who could get the smelly fish the farthest into Alabama. She described Mullet Toss as a huge weekend-long beach bash in which prizes are awarded for farthest toss, best bikini, and others. We agreed that rednecks are weird, and that it would be fun to see once, but we probably would not frequent the bar nor event.

After our short walk, I pitched my empty mug in a

trash can, but she said she would save hers.

We drove to dinner at McGuire's Irish Pub. She was noticeably unimpressed but perked up when she saw her perfectly aged and prepared two-inch-thick prime New York strip steak drenched in sautéed onions and garlic butter. For dessert, we split an enormous slice of cheesecake and an Irish Wake, their green, fruity, boozy, oversized signature drink that came with two green straws and a collectable green and white lace garter lying on top of the base of its huge goblet. She made the comment that trying to get her drunk won't work. We both smirked. She kept the garter, excited to show it off to Jolene.

After eating the best steaks in town, we drove over to Trader Jon's Pub. We got a couple of frosty lagers and were treated to a tour of the famous Blue Angel room by Trader Jon Wiseman, himself. I knew he would oblige us as he was a sucker for a pretty female face. Jill didn't disappoint. She had her shining dark hair pulled back and bumped up in the back, wore tasteful makeup and lipstick, and was decked out in a white patterned summer dress and matching white sandals. Trader Jon was a gruff, short, older gentleman who always greeted me with "What are ya drinkin'?" He called Jill my angel, his standard lady compliment and play on words. His bar was known to most as just "Trader's" and was almost as famous as the P-Cola Naval Air Station itself. He had a homemade tribute museum to the Blues in a large room open to the bar. He told a couple of short stories, but mostly pointed to pictures of himself with various members of the team, including one signed by Viper Watson. He showed us posters, helmets, blue and yellow flight suits, F-4, A-4, and F-18 models, patches, stickers, and holy hell, dice and drink coasters and all things Blue Angels.

We finished our beers and sat at a table in the corner. I offered to take her to Wrong-Way Finnegan's, the most popular dance hall that I knew of. I told her it would be crowded with SNAs and local twenty-somethings drinking and dancing, poorly, to ridiculously loud hip-hop and funk music. Thankfully, she said it wasn't really her bag, but that she would like to see the Pensacola Officer's Club some time, just not to tell her mom. I told her that I would be delighted and honored to dine with her in uniform at the club on our next date in my Harvard accent with my chin stuck out. She asked if I was being serious or sarcastic. I told her she would have to decide that for herself.

I then told her that I was being serious when I spilled the beans about Franky. She had heard there was an accident on the news but was unaware of my personal interest in the matter.

She of course said she was very sorry to hear about my instructor's misfortune and then hit me with the worst news of my week. She was leaving in three weeks for a traveling nursing job in Colorado. She had already applied to an agency months ago, but this was their first offer to travel somewhere that she wanted to go. She had given her two weeks' notice at her current job, and she had made her decision. She and Bailey were heading west to Denver.

"Well, that's just great, fantastic," I said with obvious sarcasm this time. "I meet someone intelligent, beautiful, fun, and intriguing and she plants her foot right in my balls!"

I was just getting going and really starting to fume when she grabbed my face with both of her strong hands and kissed me hard on the mouth with tongue for about five seconds.

I whimpered, "I didn't even know if you liked me."

We sat in silence for a minute or two.

I asked, "Are you seeing or involved with anyone?"

"No, I don't have a boyfriend. You?"

"No girlfriend yet, but I was hoping to change that tonight. Now, I'm not so sure."

She started with her teasing thing again. "Well, you are a pilot...and my dad says that he gives you guys planes to take on cross-country flights...and you could fly out to Denver and see me..."

"Whoa, whoa, whoa. What's your dad's name?"

"Robert Schweigert, same last name as me."

"Does he wear a gray shirt to work with a white oval patch that says Bob on it in red embroidered stitching?"

"Yes he is Big Bob, or Captain Bob, or Chief Bob I think you guys call him. But don't worry too much about that. I don't speak to him anymore, and he probably knows very little about you and certainly nothing about us."

I was now completely calm and thoroughly smitten.

We had glasses of water and talked for about an hour about our families and friends. I told her about Boulder and the University and what little I knew about the Colorado towns of Broomfield, Arvada, and Cherry Creek. They were all near Denver, and I was trying to be helpful and supportive.

I drove back to her apartment and walked her to her door.

She, I think sincerely, thanked me for a great dinner, wonderful conversation, and an enjoyable evening. I gave her a longer wet kiss and a big hug. She said she would ask me in, but it was too early for that. We would have to wait for another time.

I sang with a country twang, "What if tomorrow never comes?"

She replied with her sly smile, "Well, then neither will you."

She kissed her right finger again, but this time touched it to my lips. She looked down at the bulge in my pressed khaki shorts and giggled.

She said, "Goodniiiiiiiight," with her now signature voice.

She smiled, winked, and closed the door, leaving her honor intact and me and my erection outside.

Wow could she tease.

CHAPTER 22

BYE BYE

I noticed spots on my bathroom mirror. I made my second mental note to clean it later and I continued with my reverie.

I saw the skipper, my new on-wing, on Monday and assured him that I wanted to and was okay to fly. Over the next couple of weeks, I finished BIs and started into the most complex flying yet, Radio Instrument flights, RIs.

I sat in the back in whites at the small private funeral

service in the base chapel. The casket was closed, adding to our misery. I watched and cried as grown men and women, mostly Marines, said their tearful goodbyes and made speeches about my deceased hero. It was particularly gut wrenching to watch his wife Sarah walk her twin toddlers, Sophia and Benjamin, up to the U.S. flag-draped casket and encourage them to touch it and say "Bye bye, Daddy."

She said that Ron was a good man, a great husband, and a better father. She said that he was an English major at Tulane, where they both went to college. She knew that he loved her deeply and sacrificially and that he equally loved his children. She knew he loved flying and poetry and would sometimes read this poem as lullaby to their twins.

She stood at the casket and read with courageous dignity.

"This poem was written by John Gillespie Magee Jr., a Canadian Air Force pilot who, unfortunately, also died in a plane crash.

"High Flight

Oh! I have slipped the surly bonds of Earth

And danced the skies on laughter-silvered wings;

Sunward I've climbed, and joined the tumbling mirth

Of sun-split clouds, and done a hundred things

You have not dreamed of, wheeled and soared and swung

High in the sunlit silence. Hov'ring there,

I've chased the shouting wind along, and flung

My eager craft through footless halls of air...

Up, up the long, delirious burning blue

I've topped the wind-swept heights with easy grace

Where never lark or ever eagle flew,

And, while with silent, lifting mind I've trod

The high untrespassed sanctity of space,

Put out my hand, and touched the face of God."

She folded and tucked the paper in the flowers near the casket.

"Goodbye, darling. Dear God, keep Ronald now and forever in your peace."

Sarah started to shake and cry. Captain Wantrowski hustled over, steadied her, and helped her walk slowly back to the first pew on the left side of the altar and casket. She sat down with her small children and then the base chaplain said a closing prayer.

There were no bagpipes nor music of any kind.

Captain Wantrowski assisted Sarah and the twin children out of the chapel.

We followed in silence and sorrow.

A few days later, the Wing of three squadrons and others attended a vanilla and much less moving memorial for Capt. Franklin in the big auditorium at Pensacola main side. Admiral Watson, the commodore of the Training Wing, our LTCL Snake, and two fellow instructors spoke in glowing terms about Franky and of his dedication and heroism. He was posthumously awarded the Navy and Marine Corps Medal, the highest military peacetime decoration for valor.

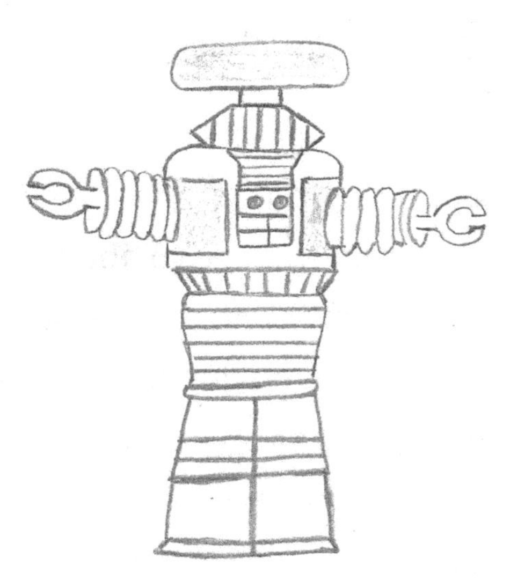

CHAPTER 23

LOST IN SPACE

Yes, the asinine sitcom with a silly robot waving his floppy arms around and up and down and saying, "Danger, danger, Will Robinson" depicted my mental ability in regard to radio instrument flying. I wasn't even the prepubescent Will Robinson. I was the idiotic, bumbling, frightened, confused, and barely mobile robot.

So much for being a prodigy. I was pretty good at all of the visual maneuvers including takeoffs, landings, and aerobatics. However, I struggled mightily with conceptually operating and flying the airplane on instruments alone. I received a two above averages total through the five BI flights, and this net score was below average for the stage. Uh oh, it was an accurate precursor of things to come. I was downed and received the aforementioned full two below averages on RI-2.

The first several hops of the RI stage were flown in a simulator. The cockpit mockup was good, and the control stick, throttle, gear and flap handles, and the damned instruments were all there and correctly positioned, but I did not know how to read nor use them. The seats of the sim were more comfortable as there was no parachute or five-point harness available nor needed. The units had no motion ability and no exterior visual cues either. I would close the canopy and be able to see nothing outside, not even shadows or flickering sunbeams poking through like when I was under the bag in the actual airplane. During RI-2, I had no geographical idea where I or the airplane was in theory. I was literally lost in simulated airspace. I did notice that the gray forward instrument panel had a stopwatch type clock and a VSI—a vertical speed indicator—registering in feet per minute. I swore that these had never been there before.

Marwinn and I commiserated my down and again thought it unfair to get downed on only the second flight in stage, yada, yada. We got that over with and I got after the task at hand. I needed to figure this stuff out or not graduate. I didn't want the boot, so asked Smarts to help me. He did and he was a few flights ahead of me in RIs, so it worked out nicely. Sure, I was sometimes frustrated and wanted to jump up and down with both fists clenched and scream, "I just want to go fast and fly upside down," like an angry four-year-old, but his patience, intelligence, and cool attitude got me through. I think he could actually translate concepts and mentally visualize his position while flying. I could not. I just needed to stay inside and make the needles and instruments work. To make matters worse, we had to make internal and external radio calls. I felt mostly like saying, "Not now, I'm busy," but I managed to read the required items from scripted statements on my kneeboard. I needed all the help I could get, and I was grateful for the classroom instruction and Smarts' tutelage throughout the stage.

The airplane's primary instrument was the altitude gyro that indicated a false horizon and the wing and nose position of the airplane. Simply, it shows if you are going up or down and/or turning. Additional instruments included the altimeter, airspeed indicator, VSI, VOR, TACAN, DME, flap and landing gear position indicators, and engine instruments...like oil pressure and temperature, fuel flow, and turbine and propeller speeds. Oh yeah, there was a clock too, up and to the left, and although critical, it was easily dropped out of one's scan.

There was also a brake pressure gauge, an oxygen gauge, and a pneumatic gauge for the emergency canopy blow and probably more.

Now, for the instrument stuff. The VOR is a VHF omnidirectional range machine. It put the tail of the VOR needle on the compass or radio magnetic indicator (RMI, one I forgot to mention) in the cockpit on the particular radial off of the VOR facility that the airplane is on. It would be one of the two-dimensional 360 radials emanating out of the actual VOR tower on the ground: 000 and 360 degrees are north, 180 is south, 90 east, and 270 west, just like on a Boy Scout or Cracker Jack compass.

The TACAN or tactical air navigation needle does the same thing and is also affixed to the RMI.

DME is distance measuring equipment and indicates one's distance from a ground VOR or TACAN navigation station in nautical miles.

Heads fall and tails rise. That is the pointy ends of said VOR and TACAN needles fall to new positions and the straight ends rise as the airplane travels along through the mirthful, radial-filled sky.

Oops, there is also a CDI, a course deviation indicator that aids in holding a radial position and deflects out on a dotted scale when one gets off course.

The challenge that aircraft controllers put to pilots is to consider all of these instruments and fly the appropriate heading, altitude, and airspeed to position the aircraft properly even though the pilot may not see a darn thing outside of his airplane.

We learned to use the instruments and more importantly their indications to fly maneuvers and patterns. We flew simulated STARS and SIDS; these are standard instrument arrivals and departures to and from airfields. We put the airplane in instrument holding patterns and executed the exits of these ovals in the sky. I still use the 6Ts to this day: time, turn, time, transition, twist, talk. Time—look at the clock and jot down the time. Turn—to the outbound intercept heading. Time—start the stopwatch because after one minute it is time to turn back inbound while holding. Transition—slow down to holding airspeed and maybe drop the gear and/or flaps if this were a holding pattern approach. Twist—set the inbound holding course in the CDI so that it can be tracked inbound after the one minute. Talk—to air traffic control and report the holding fix, the time that was scrawled on the kneeboard, altitude, and expected further clearance time given with the holding instructions by ATC at the beginning of this debacle.

We also attempted the big time. The instrument approaches that required the utmost of my concentration. We were expected fly non-precision approaches precisely. These were procedure turn, tear drop, holding pattern, circling, and straight-in VOR and TACAN approaches that got you close enough to an airport to maneuver and land the plane. There was also the precision approach radar type or PAR that a ground controller would tell a pilot over the communications radio to fly left, right, and descend on a precise glide path down to a particular runway. It felt and sounded like an old World War II movie. This one would hopefully spit you at two hundred feet above the runway on centerline and in the groove, that is on the glide slope, on centerline of the runway, and configured to land. I learned to use the VSI and found that about five hundred feet per minute down worked well on the final approach segments.

We practiced these procedures what seemed like hundreds of times. We didn't have an internal landing system on the T-34Cs, so we were spared learning ILS precision approaches for the primary flight school phase of training. The planes had no autopilots, so we flew it all manually. To make matters worse, in addition to making the navigation needles work, we had to talk on the radios and inter phone, raise and lower the flaps and gear, continuously adjust our heading, altitude, and airspeed, try to think, and complete checklists. I battled through my confusion and passed the RI-15 check flight. I made maybe eight to ten above averages total, which was about average for stage. I bought Smarts a steak dinner.

CHAPTER 24

LEAVING THE TOWN

I dated Jill almost every other day for the next three weeks. I was midway through RIs when the day came. I woke up on a queen-size air mattress in Jill's otherwise empty apartment with Bailey licking my face. It was a Saturday morning in mid-September. Jill was lying to my left and still asleep. I mused.

What a night. We gathered last night at Flounder's restaurant for a goodbye dinner for Jill. Jolene and Mark set the whole thing up. They invited Jill's friends from her old neighborhood and two nurse buddies from Jill's hospital. My horde were there too, and they enjoyed making Navy type toasts throughout the evening. Jill was embarrassed and reserved at first, but Jolene wouldn't stand for that.

Jill was genuinely moved and touched when Jolene announced that she was going to attend college. Jolene said that Jill had been hounding her for years to start, and that she would take management classes at PJC, thanks to Jilly's encouragement.

She continued, "Come on now, girl, we came to this fancy place with white table cloths for you, and I'm not lettin' my little Jilly Ree go nowhere without a proper sendoff."

I gave her a fourteen-karat gold bracelet with a small rope-fouled anchor on it as a going away gift.

Jill had steak and a bite of my scallops, which she said weren't too bad. We had key lime pie for dessert. We had a few drinks, but not too many. We all actually danced, poorly, to live music on the outdoor patio. The local band played plenty of Navy favorites like "Danger Zone," "The Wreck of the Edmund Fitzgerald" and of course "That Lovin' Feeling."

The guys picked up the dinner tab and wouldn't let me contribute. My cronies, Jolene, and her crowd sent us off in a horse-drawn carriage for the short ride back to Jill's apartment. They gave us quite a salute with poppers and ribbons and glitter and holy heck. They clapped, hooted, and hollered. Jill cried. Mark said they would take my car home and he would pick me up in a couple of hours.

It was all a setup, I suppose, and I was glad.

Jill said at the end of our carriage ride, "Why don't ya come in and help me sort me holy cards?" in her best Maggie O'Hooligan Irish accent.

I was floored, as she had never invited me in after a date before, and with a *Caddyshack* reference to boot. Really? And I was about to get lucky? Could this chick get any cooler? I answered to myself no, but the invitation inside really didn't matter. I was completely, truly, and madly in love with her already.

As I lay there, I briefly thought that having our first physical relations the night before she left was her ultimate tease. I could hear her saying, "Goodbye...call me...I'm in the book..." as she got in her car to drive to fucking Colorado. I brought myself back to reality, knowing that she liked me too and didn't intend it this way. After all, I told her that I was falling in love with her and she said, "I think I'm falling for you too."

I cleaned up a bit and walked the dog while Jill showered and dressed. Mark and Jolene showed up for final hugs and goodbyes. We deflated the air mattress and packed the last few things and Bailey in her car and small U-Haul trailer. She kissed me and promised to call from the hotel in Misery, her name for Missouri, tonight and tomorrow when she safely made it to Denver. She drove off and started her grand adventure.

Absence makes the heart grow fonder. Well maybe, but in that case I'm in big trouble because watching her leave was painful enough already. How about the song "Love Stinks"? Love conquers all. That might work, if in fact she loves me. We'll see.

"Westward ho!" I yelled as she pulled away, but hopefully not out of my life forever.

CHAPTER 25

LIGHTS

I had just returned to our apartment at 2200 after Night Fam-One. The flight was pretty easy. I was glad to get to sit in the front seat again and fly around once more under visual flight rules. The instrument training was valuable and I was benefitting from a pretty decent instrument scan in addition to looking outside. The instructor showed me the toggle for night/day. I selected night and noticed that instruments now glowed in a pleasant red hue more suitable for night flying as this would keep one's night vision more easily intact. I was approaching the end of primary training and I had just learned something new. I was just dimming the white lights for all of those night BIs and RIs. I was again humbled, but Capt. Wantrowski said, "Don't worry, not many SNAs know the switch exists." I suppose the old axiom that we learn something new every day is probably true. In that case, we never truly graduate in life, do we? I also thought that maybe I should pay more attention to each day. That maybe the journey itself is as important as the destination. Make every day great, carpe diem, woohoo.

I returned to reality and we went to the Saufley outlying field for several night touch and go landings. Mine were kind of meh. Then we just flew around and Capt. Wantrowski showed me several points of interest like NAS Pensacola and the civilian Pensacola International Airport. He showed me that pretty much every airport with a big runway would have a rotating beacon, even the one in Mobile, Alabama. He did a touch and go at International to show me the approach lighting system. We recovered at NAS Whiting, our home field in Milton.

I asked Marwinn if he knew about the day/night

switch, which was below and left of the seat in the front cockpit. He said no, but thanks for the heads up. He thought maybe he could parlay the knowledge into an above average grade. He was now in the formation stage of flying and would complete Night Fams next, and that would be the last of his primary training.

It had been a month since Jill left, and although we spoke on the phone a few times a week and we exchanged a couple of letters, I was lonesome for specifically her. I ran into Johnni in the squadron duty office as she would be SDO every other day until she healed up. She asked if we could have dinner sometime, and I regretfully told her no because I was seeing someone, even though Jill and I never made a commitment to each other. I was afraid to ask Jill if she had any suitors, but I suspected she had plenty.

I talked to my roomie Mark about possibly quitting flight school and finding some easy job in the Navy so I could be with Jill.

Marwinn went off. "Oh yeah, solid plan. Quit for some silly tart. I'm sure she would love to be with a degenerate dropout who would be freeloading off of her nursing job. Oh, and another thing, the guys that drop out mostly wind up on a ship. Do you think that driving a Navy ship would be easy? Driving a ten-thousand-ton, four-hundred-foot-long floating hunk of steel through harbors, ports, and stormy seas while freezing one's ass in the North Atlantic? They call themselves SWO daddies for the Surface Warfare Officer school they attend, and they don't even get their water wings until after school and being on the boat for over a year. Don't you remember from our ROTC summer cruises? No effing thanks, I say. Oh, and your flight grades are better than mine. So tell me why you would now elect to throw away a Naval Aviation career when you, my man, are good at it? Lastly, you're a complete idiot. If you were in SWO school and/or on a ship, you wouldn't be with her anyway. The Navy sometimes just isn't conducive to romantic relationships. Live with it, wuss. Like the commercial says, don't be a fool, stay in school!"

"All right, all right, all right. I asked for it, and you set me straight. Thanks. Jill's not a silly tart though. I find her quite fetching, and not in the canine way; it means she is charming, appealing, and pretty."

"Yeah, pretty damn snarky, and sometimes outright caustic," Mark chided.

I flew Night Fam-Two the next night, the last of the short stage. I again flew with the Polish Terror, and he was in no way like his nickname. He was relaxed, intelligent, and competent.

He debriefed our flight. "First off, very nice flight. Great night landings. You were on speed, on centerline, and in the middle of the box every time. Your overall air work was above average also. You thought ahead, put the airplane where we intended, controlled our altitude within ten feet, and pretty much nailed the airspeeds all night. Your headwork was impressive. You tuned the VOR and TACAN to Whiting, Mobile, and NAS P-Cola. This is not in the syllabus, but showed your overall awareness and attention to navigation. So, just outstanding. I am pleased to give you a well-deserved three-above hop.

"Second, as you may or may not know, Captain Franklin was a close friend of mine. My wife and I are the godparents of his two young children. I knew him well. He liked to fly with you and told me that your efforts were inspiring, showing up with your busted face and all. He said that you have natural ability and a talent for flying. Don't give up on him now; he would be proud of your development as a pilot.

"Now lastly, you have formation flying (forms) coming up. This is an intro to this type of flying. When you are the lead, be smooth and gentle. Use slow rates of roll and ease into climbs and descents. Be a stable platform that your wingman can follow easily. I know you'll nail the wingman role. You just look outside, stay on his wing using the checkpoints you'll learn about. Just control your relative motion to the lead aircraft.

"I'm telling you because I know you've seen the Blue Angels and they rip G's and accomplish inverted rolls and loops while in formation. Easy does it, our forms are not that kind of flying. Don't yank and bank. Enjoy it. It's fun. Oh, by the way, where do you think each and every Blue started out? Yep, in this same crappy briefing cubicle and maybe the exact same chair you are sitting in now. Food for thought.

"Anyway, great job tonight. That will be all."

I told my buddies that Captain Wantrowski was great to fly with, but I could see their skepticism, and I guess I deserved their incredulity. We pranked each other mercilessly and continuously. I told them about the three above averages. They didn't believe that either.

Marwinn, the Skipper, and now Wantrowski thought I had a promising career ahead of me. The girl I loved was doing well with her nursing career and had the courage to follow her dreams. She had started playing recreational softball, and was already looking forward to volleyball in the winter. I was concerned for her and relieved that she was safe. I was glad she was happy. She was talking to me about her successes and disappointments. She liked me even though I had not yet taken her to the Officer's Club as I promised. We were in the midst of a new romance and a decent long distance relationship. Maybe lights were starting to shine a little brighter for me.

CHAPTER 26

CONSTANT CHANGE

It's said that the only constant in life is change. Such is the case for the first individual and completely autonomous leadership role in the Navy and Marine Corps. The commanding officer, known colloquially as the Skipper, only holds his post for one year. This comes after a one-year stint as number two in charge, the executive officer.

Thus, on November 1, 1989, Training Squadron Three held its annual Change of Command ceremony. We were dressed in Service Dress Blues, the classic

Navy double-breasted black suit with gold buttons, ribbons, and name tags. The Marines wore their black choker top blues with royal blue pants with the thick red "blood stripe" running full length on both sides of the trousers. They opted for ribbons and gaudy full-sized medals. There were sets of gold Navy wings on uniforms everywhere. Most of us were drooling at the thought of someday getting to wear them.

This was a no-fly day for the squadron. The VT-3 hangar had been cleared out for the event and replaced with rows of hundreds of folding chairs. The dignitaries sat up front at white linen tables. Behind us and the rows of chairs was a bright and shiny T-34C Turbo Mentor, and a massive U.S. flag hanging from the rafters.

To the front was the omnipresent podium. Most of the instructors' wives and dates were in attendance, but we the students were instructed to come alone to the mandatory event for capacity concerns. Of course, Johnni sat right next to me. She looked like a beautiful professional with her olive-skinned face, tasteful make-up, and conservative lipstick, and hair up and under her white Donald Duck hat. I commented that she looked a lot better without her arm cast. She told me that her investigation was, as expected, a royal pain, but she was surviving and looked forward to flying again. She pointed to the corner of the hangar as she spoke. There was a roped-off area with chunks and pieces of their plane neatly arranged on the floor in as close to their proper positions as possible. It kind of looked like a real-life three-dimensional diagram. The investigation was ongoing and they had not yet determined the cause of the explosion.

She asked how things were going for me, pointing casually to her left cheek. I told her that I dropped the charges and I was done with that hassle. I told her that I was mostly now standing watches and only flying once a week in the squadron because the fiscal year ended and I was no longer a pilot training rate priority. It would end as it began for me, in the office. She rolled her eyes in agreement as she was also standing a ton of duties. She said the flight surgeon would return her to flying status as soon as her arm was strong enough to do ten pullups.

As for the watches, I was standing SDO, squadron duty officer, and assistant flight duty officer or AFDO. The SDO spot was tedious, but easy. I directed people around the squadron and answered the phone, mostly reading the flight schedule for SNAs. The khaki working uniform was required. The AFDO job was a flight suit job and more fun as we solely kept track of flying sorties with a slot board in the Flight Operations shack. There was more time to relax, make and drink coffee, and chat. When the skipper or any squadron officer wanted to know who was in the air, they just called the shack.

"Attention on deck" was shouted and we all stood and locked it up. We stood at attention for what seemed like an eternity as dignitaries filed in, and the National Anthem and then the Hymn of the Marine Corps were played over the loudspeakers.

Finally, Snake Collens took the podium as the first speaker and outgoing CO. He said, "At ease, ladies and gentlemen," finally. His remarks were brief as this really wasn't his big day. Yeah, yeah, yeah. Honesty, loyalty, integrity, courageous decisions, I had it, you got it, it has been my privilege, thank you, and bye now.

The ceremony was a big deal for the incoming CO, Navy Commander Alex John "Shooter" Smith. One of his old COs spoke and made a joke that Shooter was going to be nicknamed Wesson, kind of corny, he knew, but his flying wasn't that slick. The old guys chuckled and the students groaned. His old CO and then the commodore, head of our wing, spoke on CDR Smith's behalf. Yada, yada, great guy, motivated and dedicated, family man, solid pilot, team player, and friend. Phew, it was getting deep and thick.

Commander Smith then spoke. He thanked everyone from the Old and New Testaments, all of his fellow officers, and then tearfully and genuinely thanked his wife, without whom his life, profession, success, and happiness would be impossible. Of course some more yada, thanks for the great job and example, Snake, awesome past, like the direction of the current, and of course a bright and better future lies ahead. More hooray, oh yah, ooh-rah yelled by some idiot Marine, more chuckles, but sincerely, folks, he's honored and humbled to assume this post, and done.

The ninety-minute ceremony was coming to a close and I wrestled my brain. Should I ask Juanita AKA Johnni out to lunch or dinner tonight? She was humorous, intelligent, and beautiful. I would like to get to know her in a physical sense. There are religions in the world that encourage multiple partners and wives. Hmmm. Jill Marie and I really have no stated commitment to each other. Seize the day, woohoo. Marwinn wouldn't tell on me, but Jolene surely would advise her "little Jilly Ree" of my sordid behavior. Would Jill be hurt if she found out? "Aw, now why did you have to think that?" my internal Jimmy Stewart voice asked. Why did my parents raise me to have the traditional value of one man, one woman? Would either woman provide the encouragement and comfort that Shooter thanked his wife for?

"Attention on deck."

We stood at attention as the Navy hymn "Anchors Aweigh" was played. It bothers me that some don't know that it means the big hook is hanging in the water or aweigh. Presumably, it was just pulled and the ship is heading out to sea. Some think that it is "anchor's away," whatever in the hell that would mean. Maybe the rope or chain is chopped and the anchor is lost forever? I thought of Captain Franklin and how I wished he would have assumed command of a squadron.

I said goodbye to Johnni and held my arms straight but at a forty-five-degree angle downward, palms out, offering her a hug. She accepted, we enjoyed a hearty and heartfelt embrace, and she said, "Bye," most probably forever.

CHAPTER 27

PROPER FORM

I pulled my cheek to the side with my left index finger and looked in the mirror. The gum spot was still vacant. At least it didn't seem infected. On his last try, I sat in the dentist's chair hoping to have my new number nineteen installed. Was I getting a permanent denture? Maybe, who cares? I just wanted to end my endless jaw trouble.

LCDR Joseph Green first had his dental assistant give my teeth a good scraping that they called cleaning.

Then he numbed me up and removed the wire bridge over my gum hole. He said that he had seen a new procedure in which my tooth would be fastened to a post that would be completely invisible after the tooth was attached to it. I mumbled and nodded to go ahead. He drilled a hole down into my jaw bone and screwed in the post. He then, I guessed, drilled a hole in the tooth and glued it to the post. He ground on the tooth a bit and adjusted it for my bite.

I said, "Sthanks and goodbye," through my swollen, anesthetized face.

After a couple more watches, a formation class, and some healing, I flew Form-1.

The Formation phase of primary flight training started off as we always did with the classroom work first. RIs took a week of ground school, but BIs, PAs, Fams, and Forms were only a day. Halloween had come and gone, and it was now mid-November. The fiscal year had already ended, and the squadron was already pre-loading X's to make PTR.

The first flight of the stage was the typical show and tell, and the instructors demonstrated the maneuvers. We flew a two-ship formation with a lead and a wingman for the hop. We flew two as one for the departure, air work, and arrival. The whole flight was in daylight, and we looked outside continuously. It was right up my alley and rather fun. There I went enjoying flying again.

We accomplished inside and outside turns, lead changes, and under runs. The flight pretty much went as briefed with the lead being a stable platform and wingman religiously sticking to his side, forty-five degrees off and slightly behind and lower than the lead. We also flew the breakup and rendezvous, the toughest item of the sequence. We would separate a good couple of miles and then rejoin to proper formation, all the while keeping our partner in sight and controlling the rate of closure so as to not collide. I hoped to accomplish the maneuver metaphorically with Jill, but with a gentle collision at the end.

Forms Two through Four were about the same with more flying from the instructors to transition to the students. I flew all of Form-Five, my safe-for-solo check flight, as the lead.

I recalled my last solo, PA-5. Yes, this was when I messed up the banner flight pattern over the beach.

What the skipper didn't know was that I read up on how to accomplish a snap roll, also an unauthorized maneuver. Although I slowed below maneuvering air-speed, the speed slow enough that a maximum control deflection would not over G the airplane, it felt like I damn near twisted the tail off of the bird. I scared my-self as I spun upside down around the plane's longitu-dinal axis. This time I would heed Snake's words and I would not do anything out of the norm; besides, there would be a chase airplane with an instructor or two monitoring our formation.

We completed our solo formation uneventfully as Varmint flight. I was the wingman for this sortie, the more enjoyable position.

I was all smiles. I had just completed Primary Fight Training! I had just signed in my airplane after the formation solo, my last primary flight. Chief Bob ap-proached me.

He said, "Congratulations, Captain Franklin would be proud. Um, have you talked to my daughter, Jill, recently?"

He caught me off guard. I thanked him for ac-knowledging my completion and admitted that I had been speaking with her occasionally over the last few months.

He told me his neighbors, the Hatfields, had mentioned that their daughter Jolene was dating the handsome and polished Ensign Marwinn, and that the whole family liked him and the way he treated and thrilled Jolene. He said that her mother gushed when Mark bought her a new dress for Jilly's going away party, and the dad was happy that Jolene was attending college and finally motivated to do something other than work at the video rental store.

I said, "Hatfields, huh? That would explain Jolene's penchant for feuding."

He responded that she was quite a firecracker or maybe an atom bomb, but didn't think she was related to the famous feuding family.

We chuckled.

Big Bob then asked me directly, "So what do you think of Jill?"

I thought to myself that she smells as good as movie theatre popcorn. I took a moment and organized my response cautiously.

"Well, I find her a blatantly blunt, freakishly factual,

physically fit woman with the drive and confidence of a tennis star. Her perky personality sizzles with snarky sarcasm. Although she intimidates me a little, it's safe to say that I am extremely fond of her."

Bob offered, "That sure sounds like her."

He continued, "Anyway, I heard that you and Jill were friendly, and if you see or speak with her any time soon, please tell her that I love her, and that her mom and I miss her and we hope she comes home for Christmas. You're invited too, Ensign Rudd, if you're still around and Jill wants to bring you."

He smelled like stale booze, and I wondered if that was why Jill wouldn't talk about or to him. He was sniffling, wiping his nose with his enormous, off-white handkerchief, and holding back sobs.

I thanked him again and shook his hand. I told him that I hoped to see Jill Marie again and that I most certainly would pass along his invite and kind words.

He nodded, turned, and slowly walked away.

I shared his pain.

CHAPTER 28

GRADUATION

I finished on a Monday in early December. I thought the list would not come out until Friday afternoon usually around 1500. We would, of course, have a brief about selection just before at 1300. Thanks to Marwinn, I now painfully knew that Skipper Smith had made earlier arrangements, and I was pressing to make his dastardly 0800 brief.

I had FDO duty on Tuesday and Thursday, again which I enjoyed. I was genuinely liking myself and feelings of freedom generated from completion of the Primary syllabus.

My damned number nineteen fake molar with the hole in it cracked and fell out again on Wednesday. LCDR Joe Green—or Joey the Hack, as I now refer to him—removed the post and said not to worry, that he would have it all fixed up by next week. We'll see if that mobster stealing LCDR O-4 pay can at least be good to his word, and, for the love of all things big and small, get my tooth fixed!

Still looking in the mirror, I forced a smile and noted a more positive version of me. I reflected briefly about other selection Fridays. Harry and his prior flight time earned him a jet slot. Petey got props or P-3s, which was his first choice. Greg "Smarts" McSorley selected and received helos, which he thought were cool because they would never go upside down and make him puke.

I wondered what this Friday afternoon would bring for me and Marwinn. He had his last flight, Night Fam-Two on Wednesday. I know Mark made the jet cut-off for grades, and I was a little higher than him. The needs of the Navy and Marine Corps still trumped our preferences, which we submitted on "dream sheets." I asked for jets, props, E2/C2s sequentially and didn't even bother putting down my absolute last choice—helos. Please, dear God, anything but that. Maybe I could volunteer for some CIA flying or I might rather drive a ship or a tank. Considering a little over half of all naval aviators fly helicopters, the chance was real and maybe likely that they would be in our future.

I noted that my buddies received the slots they desired and seemed to have real peace regarding their immediate and favorable futures. I thought of Leo's book *War and Peace.* My high school English teacher insisted that the title was not War *or* Peace intentionally and asserted that Mr. Tolstoy knew there was always war *and* always peace. The setting for this literary masterpiece is Napoleon's invasion of Russia in the early 1800s. Before and after that, revolutionary, civil, and national wars incessantly raged around the world and still do today, but some nations were and are at peace. He also thought that a figurative war and peace could exist in one's mind. That is we could fight with our beliefs and wrestle our conscience or calm down and find peace within ourselves. Hence, even though war and peace exist simultaneously and at all times both literally on and around our globe and metaphorically within ourselves, we can choose peace. We can always find it and maybe even create it.

I left the bathroom and headed for my bedroom. I saw the clock, 0727, crap. I found a clean T-shirt, boxers, and dress socks in my dresser drawer. I went to my closet in search of a clean and pressed set of uniform khakis. I now hoped with my brain, heart, and soul that no matter what we were assigned, we would find success, satisfaction, and peace regardless of our military destinations.

Mark shouted, "It's 0730, let's go, Ruddster!"

I hollered, "I need a water."

"Got it, check," Mark responded.

I was fully dressed but carried my shoes, wallet, and dog tags in my hands. I headed for the door with anxious trepidation.

"But how bad can it really be?" I muttered to myself.

After all, it's graduation day.